Happy 4th of July MURDER

BONZAI
MOON

BonzaiMoon Books LLC
Houston, Texas
www.bonzaimoonbooks.com

This is a work of fiction. Names, characters, places and incidents either are the product of the authors' imaginations or are used fictitiously, and any resemblance to actual persons, living or dead, business establishments, events, or locales is entirely coincidental.

1

Beanie stared at his wife Noelle, a stunning West Indian beauty, and asked, "Babe … what do you think?"

"Hmmm …" Noelle squeezed the mango she'd picked from a mountain of mangoes piled in a bin and peered at the greenish, reddish, orangish fruit. "Think about what?"

"Think what!" Clapped little Evan, their two-year-old, sitting in the child seat of the grocery basket. "Think what!"

Beanie tried not to roll his eyes. His wife became single-minded when she shopped for groceries. And she was very focused and compulsive when they shopped for food provisions for the upcoming week, which was their routine on Sundays following church—provided Beanie didn't have to work at the last minute.

As an investigative reporter for the *Palmchat Gazette*, the award-winning Caribbean publication that had chronicled island news for over a hundred years, Beanie was always on call.

After changing from their Sundays best to more comfortable, casual wear, Beanie, Noelle, and the boys enjoyed an early family dinner and headed out. Normally, they visited different open-air and outdoor food markets, a chore that took several hours and left them exhausted. But since the grand opening of the new giant mega grocery store last month —Palm-Mart—they'd been able to do all of their shopping in a large warehouse on an expansive plot of land on the island's southeast side.

Beanie wasn't sure how he felt about the new Palm-Mart—an ambitious venture founded and developed by a member of the powerful Pourciau banking dynasty. Of course, he appreciated the benefits to the St. Killian economy. But the travel time bothered him. In Beanie's opinion, driving nearly three hours round trip was too labor intensive. And he found the atmosphere of the mega grocery store lacked warmth and personality. At smaller, locally owned markets, he knew the proprietors and enjoyed gossiping and catching up with them and their families. Noelle loved the convenience and variety of Palm-Mart. It was one-stop shopping. Everything they needed was in one place. They didn't have to trek from the meat market to the fish market to the vegetable farmer's market while unsuccessfully trying to corral a sneaky, rambunctious four-year-old and a moody toddler who could go from happy and content to grumpy without warning or reason.

"Can you grab me a plastic bag, babe?" requested Noelle.

Beanie yanked one from the dispenser near a giant bin of oranges, used his index finger and thumb to open the thin plastic, and handed it to his wife. "So, what do you think about going?"

"Going where?" asked Noelle, dropping a mango—one that had passed muster—into the bag.

Sighing, Beanie said, "Going to—"

"Daddy, do we need bananas?" inquired four-year-old Ethan as he ran up to Beanie, cradling several bunches.

Frowning slightly, Beanie glanced down at his oldest son. The last time he'd checked, Ethan had been sitting beneath the basket.

Beanie resolved to keep a better eye on Ethan, a little escape artist prone to disappearing acts. The idea of Ethan getting lost in a giant grocery store sent a flurry of panic through Beanie. Not because he was afraid of losing sight of his son. He was used to Ethan running off. Beanie was more terrified of Noelle.

The one thing she didn't like about Palm-Mart was how easy it would be for someone to kidnap one of their kids without them realizing it. After all, Palm-Mart was huge, crowded, and had a complex, confusing maze-like layout. And the employees, primarily young island teenagers, didn't seem to care or want to be bothered.

"Yes, we need bananas but not that many," said Beanie, extracting one of the bunches from his oldest son. "Go put the rest back."

"Are you sure, Daddy?" Ethan gave him a skeptical glare.

"Yes, Bud, I'm sure," said Beanie, fluffing his son's curly fauxhawk. "Go put the rest of the bananas back where you got them."

"Okay, Daddy!" Ethan pivoted and took off.

"Don't run!" warned Beanie, doubtful his son heard him and knowing that even if he had, Ethan probably wouldn't have complied with Beanie's orders.

"You do know that you have to tell him not to run before he starts running, right?" asked Noelle, putting the mango she held back on the pile and picking up another one.

Beanie tried not to bristle at his wife's know-it-all tone. He knew, just as well as she did, how rambunctious and recalcitrant Ethan could be. But, historically, he and Noelle adopted different parenting styles. Noelle was a disciplinarian and a "smother." Beanie was more inclined to let the boys be boys, within reason, of course.

"Okay, so what about the 4th of July party?" asked Beanie. "You want to go?"

Grabbing another mango, Noelle glanced at him. "What 4th of July party?"

Beanie pinched the bridge of his nose. "Larry's new girlfriend—"

"What? Wait. Larry has a new girlfriend?" asked his wife, a hint of malicious glee in her tone. "What about his fiancée? What was her name? Deborah?"

"Danielle."

"That's right. Danielle," said Noelle. "What happened to her? Was she cheating? Was he cheating? Did she keep the ring?"

Beanie shrugged. "All I know is they broke up. Why, I have no idea."

"You have no idea?" asked Noelle, giving him a look. "Why am I not surprised?"

"Not surprised!" Little Evan clapped his hands and rocked from side to side. "Not surprised!"

"Well, it's not like Larry, and I discussed it at length," said Beanie. "I don't think he told me. I found out from Robyn."

"I'll bet your sister knows all the details about the breakup," said Noelle, picking up a different mango and squeezing the flesh. "Not that she would tell me. Probably wouldn't take my call. Not that I want to call her."

Beanie said nothing. No love was lost between his loving wife and his fraternal twin sister. Noelle and Robyn couldn't stand each other for reasons Beanie didn't want to think about at four o'clock on a lazy Sunday afternoon. Over the years, he'd tried to coax the women toward rapprochement, but they'd both resisted. His sister and his wife remained stubbornly reluctant to repair their relationship.

"You want to go?"

"When is it?" asked Noelle, meandering over to the next bin filled with kiwis.

"Elle?" Beanie gave his wife a look. "It's a 4th of July party."

"Oh, yeah, right," said Noelle, tossing a kiwi up and down. "Um … where is the party going to be?"

"Mommy!" Evan clapped and reached for the kiwi. "Mommy!"

"At Mango Beach," said Beanie. "Larry's new girlfriend is throwing the party."

"Mango Beach …" echoed Noelle, waving a kiwi in front of Evan, who giggled and grasped at the fruit.

"Yeah," said Beanie.

"Why does she want to have a party on the 4th of July?" asked Noelle, kissing Evan on his little nose.

"She's American," said Beanie. "And a little homesick, so—"

"Daddy, do we need a broom?" Ethan ran toward Beanie, brandishing the broom like a little West Indian Harry Potter, albeit without the black specs.

"A broom?" asked Beanie, bracing himself, worried Ethan might decide to wield the broom like a Light Saber. "Why would we need a broom?"

Dragging the broom back and forth across the grocery store's polished concrete floor, Ethan said, "Because Granny said we need a broom."

"Granny said we need a broom?" asked Noelle, a hint of annoyance in her tone.

Granny was the boys' grandmother, Noelle's mom, Natalie.

"She said the floors are always so dusty, and she told her friend, Ms. Judy, that Mommy don't ever clean the house," said Ethan as he twirled in a circle, swinging the broom around him. He ignored the shoppers nearby, many of whom hurried out of Ethan's way and gave Beanie dirty looks.

"Mommy don't clean," said little Evan, clapping his hands in delight. "Mommy don't clean!"

"Granny said me and Evan is going to get allergies!"

Concerned that Ethan might hit an unsuspecting customer, Beanie grabbed the broom. "We don't need this."

Ethan looked up at him. "Is that true, Daddy? Me and Evan going to get allergies?"

"No, you're not going to get allergies," said Noelle, lips pursed as she slammed several kiwis into the plastic bag.

"Are you sure, Mommy?" asked Ethan. "Because Granny said there is a lot of dust in the house."

Knowing that his wife was *thisclose* to exploding, Beanie took Ethan's hand and said, "We'll go put back this broom that we definitely don't need."

"But, Daddy, Granny said—"

"C'mon, Buddy, let's go."

2

"Can you believe my mother said my house was dusty?" asked Noelle, taking a sip of her cocktail, a watermelon blueberry spritzer featuring white rum. Poured into a martini glass, it was garnished with strawberries and finished with salt around the rim.

Sitting on their blanket spread over the powdery white sands of Mango Beach, Beanie sighed. He couldn't believe that, two weeks later, Noelle was still upset about her mother's assessment regarding the cleanliness of their modest home in Oyster Farms, a quiet, well-kept neighborhood of working-class St. Killians.

The day after their shopping trip to Palm-Mart, Noelle confronted her mom. Natalie apologized and claimed Ethan had taken her words out of context. Noelle had forgiven her mother. Or, so Beanie had thought. Obviously, he'd been wrong. Obviously, Noelle was still nursing a grudge the way Beanie was nursing his spritzer. He didn't like fruity drinks. And something about the combination of rum and watermelon didn't work for him. What he wanted was a Felipe beer.

"The house is not dusty," insisted Noelle.

Swaying to the sounds of steel drums vibrating from a radio, Beanie surveyed the beach.

Twenty feet away, Larry's new girlfriend's 4th of July bash was still going strong hours after it had started. The fifty plus guests laughed, drank, ate, danced, and continued to have a great time as the sun sank into the horizon, leaving behind a coppery orange sky.

Beanie and Noelle had arrived an hour after the festivities began. Their hostess, a petite blonde with a pixie hairstyle that reminded Beanie of Tinkerbell, squealed in delight upon meeting them. As he and Noelle filled paper plates with food, Beanie thought it was a nice day for a beach bash. The sun was hot and intense, but the ocean breezes tempered the heat, driving away the humidity. Ultra-white popcorn clouds dotted the intense blue sky. The smell of sizzling goat paired well with the fresh salty sea scent. The atmosphere was festive and upbeat. He'd been glad Noelle had agreed to join him.

Now he wondered if his wife had really been in the mood to have a good time.

"And then she had the audacity to imply that I would put my children's health at risk."

Shielding his eyes from the late afternoon sun, Beanie scanned the buffet table—a makeshift wooden picnic table—and spotted a large cooler beneath it.

"And she's one to criticize," continued Noelle, readjusting her straw sunhat, which sported a turquoise sash around the crown that matched her bathing suit. "There's a reason she's never gotten a World's Best Mom mug from me."

Beanie didn't want to encourage a discussion of the issues his wife had with her mother.

Their problems stemmed from Natalie's bad parenting skills. Noelle resented her mother's lack of involvement in the formative years of her life. Natalie's absentee mothering led to Noelle's bad choices—including the disastrous decision she'd made to join the PC-5, a notorious island cartel responsible for most of the crime and corruption on the island. As a result, grudges lingered between mother and daughter. Disagreements escalated into fractious confrontations. His wife's relationship with her mother was tricky,

Beanie had learned. Things between them were great—until they weren't.

"Think I'm going to get a beer," said Beanie. "You want anything?"

Staring toward the ocean, Noelle shook her head.

After giving his wife a quick kiss on her forehead, Beanie stood and headed toward the beach. He wondered if maybe he should get the beer to go. Give his apologies to Larry and then suggest to Noelle that they leave early and head home. Noelle would protest, but Beanie would insist. His wife didn't seem to be in the mood for a party. Things would only get more festive as the night wore on, so—

"Excuse me ..."

Startled, Beanie turned.

About four feet behind him, three men ambled around a sand dune and walked toward him. In the waning coppery glow of the St. Killian sunset, he could tell they were older guys. Not elderly. More his parents' age. Maybe in their mid-sixties. The guy in the middle, a grossly obese fair-skinned Palmchatter, was flanked on either side by smaller men. Slight and medium height, but not frail, they were West Indian, also. The guy on the left wore a Panama hat while the man on the right had on a T-shirt with the logo of the Aerie Islands Starfish—the Palmchat Islands' main rival in the sport of cricket.

"Yes ...?" asked Beanie as the men slowed to stop a few feet away.

"You know the Mango Cove neighborhood?" asked the man in the Panama hat. "Can we get there from this beach?"

"Why are you bothering this man?" demanded the obese guy.

Shaking his head, Beanie said, "Actually, it's no bother—"

"I'm trying to make sure we're going the right way," answered the Panama hat guy.

"I told you I know the way," snapped the old coot in the Aerie Islands Starfish T-shirt.

"We been walking for a long time, and we ain't got there yet," said the man in the Panama hat.

"We're going the right way," said the obese man.

The old guy in the T-shirt cursed under his breath, waved a

dismissive hand, and then walked off, passing Beanie, who glanced over his shoulder and saw the man disappear into a narrow path between clusters of tall beach grass.

"Now look what you gone and done, Dennis," said the obese man. "You upset him."

"I don't care," said Dennis, the Panama hat guy. "I don't want to get lost out here. Going to be dark soon. I don't want to be out here at night."

"Your friend was going the right way," said Beanie. "If you follow that path he took, you should get to one of the paved roads, and you'll be in Mango Cove."

"Thank you very much," said Dennis.

"No worries," said Beanie.

"Sorry to have bothered you," said the fat man.

Chuckling to himself, Beanie watched the two men lumber onto the path, grumbling, and snipping at each other as they headed between the tall beach grass.

Moments later, Beanie reached the picnic table on the beach, where his cousin Larry and several friends gathered around a large plastic box.

"What's going on?" Beanie asked as he crouched next to the cooler and grabbed a Felipe beer.

"Fireworks!" someone yelled, which set off a chain reaction of raucous cheers, joyous whoops, and enthusiastic clapping.

"You want to help light some?" asked Larry. "We're setting them off as soon as the sun goes down."

Beanie glanced toward the horizon. The sun had already dipped below the water. Wouldn't be long—maybe another fifteen or twenty minutes—before it set.

"Yeah, I think I'll pass," said Beanie, taking a sip of his beer. Larry and his friends removed the firecrackers from the box with an excited glee that reminded Beanie of his boys opening their presents on Christmas morning.

"C'mon, man!" cajoled a few of Larry's friends. "Don't you want to light up the night sky?"

"Rockets red glare, dude!" said another guy, howling his delight, which prompted Larry's girlfriend and her friends to dance in a circle. Holding sparklers in one hand and a cocktail in the other, the bikini-clad women twirled around, singing off-key to the latest song by CoCo, the superstar recording artist and Palmchat Island native.

"I don't think so," said Beanie, sensing that their excitement was fueled more by the alcohol they'd consumed than any enthusiasm for fireworks. "Noelle would kill me if a firecracker exploded in my face."

Larry laughed, punching Beanie's shoulder. "Man, is that what marriage is like? Avoiding stuff that your wife doesn't want you to do?"

Beanie chuckled and took a sip of beer. "It's more like doing what your wife tells you to do … or else."

Larry cackled. "Or else, it's the couch for you, right? Man, I'm glad I got a girlfriend."

"Well, I'm glad I got somebody to take care of me when I get old," countered Beanie.

"Got a long time before you get old," retorted Larry, punching Beanie's shoulder again. "Long time of doing what you're told!"

Beanie shook his head as his cousin, and the other guys laughed.

"Man, you know I'm just messing with you," said Larry. "You got a beautiful family. And I don't blame you for marrying Noelle. She's a beautiful girl …"

Following his cousin's stare, Beanie glanced over his shoulder. His breath caught, and a fluttering started in his chest as he gazed at his lovely wife.

Larry said, "Shame she don't see all that good …"

Frowning, Beanie stared at Larry. "What are you talking about? Noelle has twenty/twenty vision."

"I find that hard to believe," said Larry. "If she could see that good, she never would have married you!"

Beanie had to laugh. "You've got jokes today, huh?"

Leaving Larry and his drunk friends to their task of building the fireworks, Beanie trudged across the fine sand back to Noelle. Easing down onto the blanket, Beanie pulled Noelle into his arms and kissed her forehead.

"You came back," said Noelle, moving her head to look at him.

Confused, Beanie shook his head. "What do you mean?"

"I figured you left because I was being such a wet blanket," said Noelle. "I'm sorry …"

"It's okay," said Beanie, kissing his wife's cheek. "I know how your mom gets on your nerves."

"But I shouldn't let what she said ruin my good time," said Noelle. "I shouldn't even still be thinking about what she said. Why do I even care what she thinks?"

"You care because she's your mom," said Beanie. "Kids never outgrow wanting to make their parents proud."

"You're right," said Noelle. "I shouldn't take what she says to heart. Shouldn't see it as an attack on my parenting and homemaking skills."

"No, you shouldn't," agreed Beanie, tightening his embrace around his wife as the sun disappeared.

As though on cue, Larry and his friends started the show.

For the next half hour, the sky above them served as the canvas for a dazzling light show. With his wife, Beanie enjoyed the staccato popping of conventional firecrackers interspersed with the distant boom of fireworks launched into the night sky. The fireworks streamed toward the heavens with a high-pitched whistle, spinning rapidly, shooting multi-colored sparks. More fireworks followed, flying into the clouds before bursting into a colorful globe-shaped display of sparkling lights.

"Oh, we should have brought the boys!" Noelle said.

Several fireworks burst overhead, booming loudly, creating starbursts of dazzling color.

Nodding, Beanie said, "Yeah, they would have—"

Three muted bangs behind him made Beanie pause. Frowning, he glanced back toward the clusters of sand dunes.

"Only problem is Ethan would have insisted on lighting the firecrackers, but—"

"Babe, did you hear that?"

Noelle glanced at him. "The fireworks?"

"I don't think it was fireworks," said Beanie, glancing back again.

"What do you think it was?" asked Noelle.

A strange chill passed through Beanie as he stared at his wife. "Sounded like … gunshots."

3

"Gunshots?" asked Noelle, skepticism in her tone. "Are you sure?"

"Elle, I know the sound of gunfire," said Beanie, staring at the clusters of beach grass and sea oats, trying to peer through the tall blades swaying in the ocean breeze. "I work the Handweg beat, remember?"

Handweg Gardens, an economically impoverished, crime-ridden neighborhood, was known for its gang violence. Beanie had seen more than his fair share of dead bodies while working in the dangerous enclave. And once or twice, while interviewing witnesses, he'd heard the distant, distinct report of gunfire—the same sound he'd heard moments ago.

Moonlight cast a hazy, silvery glow across the dunes, but Beanie didn't see anything other than shadows. Although, he wasn't sure what he was looking for. Evidence of the gunshots? Or maybe reassurance that he'd been wrong?

"I know you know what a gunshot sounds like," said his wife. "But, I think it was—"

A rapid-fire fusillade of firecrackers burst out, followed by a few more booming fireworks and a couple of bottle rockets.

"Now, that sounded like a PC-5 gang war," said Noelle after the barrage ceased, leaving behind laughter, conversation, and lively calypso music from the speakers beneath the picnic table.

"Yeah, I guess," said Beanie, though he wasn't exactly sure.

"Roland," said Noelle, placing a hand on his cheek, forcing him to look at her. "Maybe you did hear gunshots."

Shaking his head, Beanie said, "Or, maybe I didn't. I don't know."

"It's possible," said Noelle, scooting away from him toward her large beach bag. Filled with enough stuff to make it as heavy as a sandbag, it was suitable for weighing down the edge of their blanket. "And if it was a gun, I'll bet somebody was shooting because it's the fourth of July. Like how people shoot guns on New Year's Eve, you know?"

"You're probably right," said Beanie. "Can't stand when people do that. It's dangerous. Those bullets they shoot up into the sky always come back down, but no one thinks of that. People have been hurt, even killed, by falling bullets."

"Hopefully, they were shooting in some unpopulated area at the other end of the beach," said Noelle, delving an arm into the bag.

"What are you looking for?"

"My phone," said Noelle. "Can't find it ... hope I didn't leave it in the car."

"Who do you need to call?"

Noelle stared at him. "Who do I need to call? Are you serious? I need to check on the boys. We've been gone for hours. Have to make sure they're okay."

"They're with my parents," said Beanie. "They're fine."

"I'm sure they are, but I'd still like to make sure," said his wife, removing the contents from the bag and placing them on the blanket. "You never know. What if they've been trying to call us? I don't have my phone. They might have left a dozen messages."

"Babe, if anything was wrong and my parents couldn't reach us," said Beanie, wary of and wearied by the escalating panic in his wife's voice, "then they'd call Larry. They know where we are."

"Larry's been drinking all day," snapped Noelle. "Probably wouldn't even hear his phone."

"Noelle—"

"Where is your phone?"

Beanie hesitated and said, "It's in the glove compartment."

Noelle glared at him. "What is it doing in the glove compartment?"

"I don't know, I just—"

"Forget it," snipped Noelle. "Can you go and see if I left my phone in the car, please."

Frustrated by the shrill panic in his wife's tone, Beanie exhaled under his breath and rose to his feet. As he trudged toward the sand dunes, Beanie sighed and cursed under his breath. He should have figured that locking his phone in the glove compartment was a bad idea. But he'd wanted to enjoy the party without being bothered by any interruptions.

Beanie continued to walk, kicking up a fine spray of sand around his ankles with each step.

He'd wanted to have a good time and not worry about being called away to cover breaking news. Never occurred to him that his parents might be trying to call them because something bad had happened. Sure, he knew that anything could happen, particularly with two rambunctious boys, one of whom was reluctant to follow instructions and didn't like to behave. But if God forbid, there was an emergency, he'd figured his mother would call Noelle.

But he'd never thought his wife would have accidentally left her phone in the car.

Grumbling, Beanie continued his trek, skirting through several clusters of flowering Seaside Goldenrod spread over the sand.

He wasn't surprised that Noelle had switched—like a light—into "smother" mode.

His wife could always be counted on to overreact and become overprotective of their boys. When he pointed out her behavior, she became defensive and accused him of mocking her because she cared about her kids. That wasn't true, of course. Beanie never mocked his wife's overprotectiveness. He understood it. But he didn't think it was necessary. Not that he was an advocate of free-range parenting. But, he believed the boys had to be given a measure of freedom to be wild little boys.

Approaching the dunes, he trudged up the front slip face, carefully navigating the mound of sand and then down the back slope, veering right between dense waist-high beach grass. The path curved left and then right again before it gave way to a weather-beaten wooden plank boardwalk that ended at a narrow road.

Stepping onto warm asphalt, Beanie walked to his car.

Inside, beneath the interior lights, he searched the front and back seats for Noelle's phone. Ten minutes later, he still couldn't find it. After searching in the front and rear footwells, beneath the seats, and in the trunk, Beanie sighed.

Maybe Noelle had left her phone at home. Beanie rubbed his jaw. Well, at least he had his phone. Reaching into the glove compartment, he removed the phone and pressed the button to turn it on.

Nothing happened.

Frowning, Beanie pressed the button again. Once more, the phone didn't respond. Was the battery dead? He shook his head. The charger was at home. He was sure of that. Exhaling, Beanie shoved the phone into his pocket and then closed the car door.

Noelle was going to have a conniption, thought Beanie, heading back to the beach. He would have to borrow Larry's phone. Beanie hurried across the narrow wooden boardwalk and stepped onto the sandy path snaking through the beach grass. Striding purposefully, he tried not to allow his wife's paranoia to influence his thoughts. Nothing bad had happened with the boys. Beanie was sure of that. And yet, a niggling, annoying thought bothered him. Tried to make him worry for nothing.

Beanie hurried, anxious to get back to Noelle. The path seemed narrower. The grass taller. He recalled it being waist-high, but the thin blades on either side of him reached his shoulder. Ahead, the faint glow from the lanterns and hurricane globes on the picnic table seemed to be off to his right. When he was headed to the car, Beanie recalled looking back toward the party, and the festivities were to his left. Had he ventured onto another path? Beanie supposed so but guessed it didn't matter. The sandy paths through the beach grass growing on the dunes were like a maze, but they each led back to the beach, so—

Beanie's foot banged against something.

Before he knew what was happening, Beanie's left heel sank into the sand as his toes hooked beneath a solid, unmoving object. He stumbled slightly, trying not to fall as soft sand surrounded his ankle.

Cursing, Beanie planted his right foot and yanked his left foot, but he pulled too quickly and ended up pitching forward. He grabbed a handful of beach grass, but the slippery blades didn't stop him from losing his balance.

He fell to one knee, arms outstretched, hoping to break his fall and avoid a mouthful of sand, but—

His knee slammed against something hard and yet pliable. Something that shifted slightly beneath his weight. What had he fallen on top of? A small animal came to mind as Beanie scrambled away from the object. With both knees in the sand, Beanie leaned forward.

Faint moonlight peeked through the grass. As his eyes adjusted to the shadowy darkness, Beanie stared at the object in disbelief.

Extending from the thicket of beach grass was an outstretched arm

...

4

"How did you get blood all over you?" demanded Detective Philippi Janvier.

Glancing down at his T-shirt, Beanie frowned at the faint smears on the pale-yellow fabric.

He disagreed with the detective's assessment. There wasn't blood all over him, but Beanie wasn't surprised by Janvier's exaggeration. Regarding the man's suspicious, smug sneer, Beanie figured the detective would make more out of the blood than was necessary.

Detective Janvier—not exactly one of St. Killian's finest, in Beanie's opinion, which he would admit was biased—had a history of jumping to the wrong conclusion in his misguided zeal to collar a suspect as quickly as possible.

"That was not a rhetorical question, Reporter Bean," said the detective. "Why is there blood on your shirt?"

Beanie sighed. He was quite sure the first responders had relayed his statement to Janvier. When the detective arrived at the beach, twenty minutes after the police arrived, he'd conferred with the deputies. He appeared to be interrogating them. The deputies spoke at length, and several times, they pointed toward Beanie or inclined their heads in his direction.

Beanie figured Janvier already knew the answer to his question.

Nevertheless, Beanie explained to the detective how he'd run back to the beach after finding the dead body in the tall grass. He'd told Noelle what he'd seen, and the two of them flagged down Larry, who'd been dancing at the water's edge with his girlfriend. With his cousin's smartphone, Beanie called 911.

The other guests, somber and sobered by Beanie's grim, disturbing discovery, crowded around the picnic table, whispering their confusion and speculations. There was debate about whether or not a group should head into the dunes to investigate. There was concern that the person the arm belonged to might be hurt. Beanie ended the debate when he told the others he'd checked the person's wrist and neck for a pulse but found none.

He'd gotten the blood on his T-shirt when he'd touched the forearm, which was bare and coated with something wet and sticky. Figuring it was blood, Beanie had unthinkingly swiped his fingers across the T-shirt.

Eyes narrowed, Janvier asked, "Is there anyone who can corroborate your version of events?"

"Well, no, but—"

"So with no one to confirm that the deceased was, in fact, dead when you stumbled upon him," said Janvier, "How am I supposed to believe that you are telling the truth? How do I know that you didn't kill the dead man? Perhaps, you shot him—"

"So, he was shot?" asked Beanie, seizing on the detective's information slip.

"Twice in the gut," said Janvier. "But, perhaps you are already aware of that fact."

"How would I know that the victim had been shot?"

"Because maybe you shot him."

"I don't believe this …" Shaking his head, Beanie glanced toward the picnic table. Thirty feet away, Noelle, Larry, and a smattering of the remaining party guests huddled together, talking and glancing in his direction. Noelle appeared especially worried. When Janvier had insisted on speaking to Beanie away from the other partygoers, his wife protested.

Janvier rebuffed Noelle, giving her a cold look.

Beanie knew his wife didn't want him talking to Janvier alone, without a witness or legal representation. Her concern stemmed from past experiences with the detective. Several years ago, Janvier accused Noelle of a horrific crime she hadn't committed. Janvier maintained his staunch belief in Noelle's guilt, even in the face of overwhelming evidence to the contrary.

Noelle didn't want Janvier to railroad Beanie.

He'd told his wife not to worry.

Now he wondered if he shouldn't have been so quick to dismiss his wife's fears.

"It's not out of the realm of possibility," said Janvier. "You could have shot the dead man and then pretended to find the body to throw suspicion away from yourself."

Chuckling, Beanie said, "I didn't kill the man. Why would I? I have no idea who he is."

"I will determine whether or not you should be arrested for murder."

Exhaling his frustration, Beanie asked, "Any more questions for me?"

"Not at the moment," said Janvier. "But I reserve the right to interrogate you at a later date should the need arise—that is, should evidence come to light which connects you to the murder."

"Well, then, I have a few questions for you."

"No comment," said Janvier.

"But you didn't hear the question."

"I don't need to hear the question to know that I shall not comment upon it," said the detective.

Beanie rubbed his eyes. "Why am I not surprised?"

"Reporter Bean, I understand that you may be assigned to cover this unfortunate crime; however, I would be remiss if I did not insist and demand that you refrain from obstructing justice with your unnecessary investigative reporting."

"I don't plan to obstruct justice," said Beanie. "However, I do plan to investigate this case to make sure you capture the correct suspect."

"Are you suggesting that I will not catch the murderer?"

"Well, you've been wrong before," said Beanie, unable to help himself. "As a matter of fact, you've never been right."

"I beg your pardon," huffed Janvier, his chin lifted as he glared at Beanie with haughty rebuke.

"You can never get past your confirmation bias," said Beanie. "You decide on a suspect based on circumstantial evidence, and you look for clues to prove that you're right—even when you're wrong. Just like you did with my wife."

"Ah-ha!" Janvier's chuckle held no traces of mirth. "You are still upset because I arrested your wife, I see. Hmm. I would have thought you had gotten past that by now."

"You put my wife through the wringer," said Beanie, his anger increasing as memories of his wife's ordeal resurfaced. "And for what? Nothing. She was innocent. Not that you cared."

"She was innocent of that crime, yes," agreed Janvier, glancing toward the picnic table. "But certainly guilty of others, no?"

Frowning, Beanie asked, "What are you talking about?"

Janvier looked at him, malicious bemusement in his gaze. "Perhaps you should ask your wife …"

5

"The victim's name was Gavin de Grac," said Officer Damon Fields.

Sitting at the small desk in his tiny cubicle at the *Palmchat Gazette*'s offices, Beanie turned to his computer, grabbed his mouse, and opened a Word document. Several days had passed since Beanie had discovered the dead body in the sand dunes. After writing the initial story, which listed the basic facts, Beanie hoped to get additional details for a follow-up article.

"A sixty-three-year-old Palmchatter," continued Fields, a dedicated, veteran police deputy who was a source and a good friend. "Two bullets to the abdomen. Murder weapon was recovered in the dunes. The gun was a Glock belonging to Stanley Iris."

"Stanley Iris." Beanie typed the name into his notes. "Is he a suspect?"

"Janvier thinks so," said Fields.

"What do you think?" asked Beanie, wary that Janvier had already jumped to the wrong conclusion.

"You won't believe this," began Fields. "But I think Janvier might be right this time."

Beanie stopped typing and stared at his phone. "You're kidding."

"Turns out that Stanley Iris and Gavin de Grac have beef," explained

Fields. "And it goes way back. The two are neighbors in Seashell Estates. Their conflict stems around a palm tree."

Beanie frowned as he typed. "A palm tree?"

Fields said, "Apparently, the palm tree is planted in de Grac's backyard, but it's overgrown and needs pruning, according to Mr. Iris, because the fronds, which are limp and half dead, again, according to Mr. Iris, hang over into Mr. Iris' backyard."

"I see," said Beanie, leaning back in his chair.

"Because the tree is unhealthy," said Fields, "the fronds fall off and into Mr. Iris' pool. Mr. Iris has actually called the police several times about this issue. We got dozens of nuisance reports from Mr. Iris against Gavin de Grac. Iris complained that de Grac wouldn't do anything about the tree. Refused to take care of it. Wouldn't cut it. And wouldn't consent to Iris cutting down the tree. Problem is, there's not really anything we can do."

"Mr. Iris should bring the issue to the attention of his Homeowner's Association," said Beanie.

"That's what we told him," said Fields. "But, the last few times Mr. Iris filed a police report, he informed the officers who took the call that if the cops didn't do anything, he would take the matter into his own hands."

Beanie rubbed his jaw. "And you think Mr. Iris took the matter into his own hands? He got tired of de Grac refusing to cut down the palm tree, so he killed him? That seems a little extreme."

"Well, normally, I would agree," said Fields. "But Stanley Iris is sort of an extreme neighbor."

Typing again, Beanie asked, "What do you mean?"

"He's not the kind of guy you want to live next to," said Fields. "Iris has a record. He's attacked other neighbors before. He's got several assault and battery charges. Even spent a few years in Tiverton for attempted murder after he beat a neighbor with a shovel."

"A shovel ..." Beanie's fingers paused over the keys as memories invaded his mind. He went back in time to the horrible moment when his wife had been accused of murdering someone with a shovel, a crime she hadn't committed, that she could never have committed. But Janvier thought differently. The detective was convinced of Noelle's guilt. Janvier had been wrong, but he'd never admitted his mistakes or—

Another memory forced its way into his head, demanding his attention.

Actually, Janvier had acknowledged he was wrong about Noelle. He'd done so in a backhanded way, which allowed him to insinuate that Noelle was guilty of another crime. Beanie had bruised Janvier's ego by bringing up the detective's abysmal arrest record. In retaliation, Janvier tried to get under Beanie's skin. The detective was referring to Noelle's former gang ties, Beanie figured.

And yet, part of Beanie wondered, what if the man had been referring to some other infarction Noelle had committed? A crime Beanie had no knowledge of …?

" … threatening him," said Fields.

Shaking his head, trying to clear the disturbing memories and notions clouding his mind, Beanie asked, "What was that? Sorry. I missed what you just said."

"de Grac's cell phone was in his pocket the night you discovered his body," said Fields. "We checked out the phone. There were text messages on de Grac's phone from Iris."

"Threatening messages?"

Fields said, "Mr. Iris told Mr. de Grac that he wanted the palm tree gone or he would kill Mr. de Grac and bury his body beneath it …"

6

"Doggone skippy right. I wanted that fool dead," groused Stanley Iris, standing in the middle of his perfectly manicured lawn which featured immaculately pruned fruit trees and bushes trimmed with precision. His porch was decorated with hibiscus plants. The large, vivid pink petals looked healthy and vibrant, obviously nurtured by someone with a natural green thumb. Beanie understood why Mr. Iris had become frustrated and angered by Gavin de Grac.

Beanie asked, "Did you shoot Mr. de Grac?"

"My lawyer told me not to talk to nobody," said Mr. Iris. "Especially not no reporter."

"But you are talking to me," Beanie pointed out. "You just admitted that you wanted Mr. de Grac dead."

"Wanting somebody dead and killing them ain't the same thing," said Mr. Iris.

"So you didn't kill him?"

"My lawyer told me not to talk to nobody about what I did or didn't do," said Mr. Iris.

Annoyed by the man's stubborn resistance, Beanie said, "Well, you sent him a text threatening to kill him."

"He deserved to die," said Iris.

"Because he wouldn't cut down a palm tree?"

"Because he neglected that tree," said Mr. Iris, pale blue eyes flashing with rage. "You ain't suppose to treat nature with disrespect. You ain't suppose to let a tree die like that and not even try to help it. That tree was sick. And that fool was just gonna let it die!"

"And that's why you killed him?"

"Didn't kill nobody."

"But you sent a text message saying that you would bury him under the palm tree."

"Wasn't serious," mumbled Iris, spraying the middle tomato plant. "Just trying to scare the old fool."

"Sort of like you scared your neighbor that you nearly beat to death with a shovel?"

Beanie wasn't surprised when Iris glared at him.

"That fool needed some sense knocked into him," said Iris. "Anybody would have done the same thing I did."

"And what about what you did to Mr. de Grac? You really think anybody else would have shot him because he wouldn't cut down a palm tree?"

"I didn't kill de Grac."

"But your gun was found near Mr. de Grac's dead body," said Beanie.

"Tell you what I told the police," said Mr. Iris. "Me and de Grac got into it a few weeks ago. I pulled my gun on de Grac, but he rushed me. We tussled, and he ended up taking the gun. Told me he was keeping it so I wouldn't never be able to point it at him again."

"So you're saying that Mr. de Grac took your gun?"

Nodding, Mr. Iris said, "And I haven't seen that gun since then. So I couldn't have shot him with it."

"Did you tell the police that?"

"They didn't believe me," said Mr. Iris. "Said I have no proof that de Grac took my gun. And I didn't report the gun stolen."

"Why not?"

"Because they weren't going to do nothing," grumbled Mr. Iris. "Just like they didn't do nothing about that tree hanging over the fence into my yard!"

Beanie asked, "Do you have an alibi for the night Mr. de Grac was murdered?"

"Was here at the house by myself," said Mr. Iris. "But I don't have any way to prove that, either, so as far as the police is concerned, I don't have an alibi. But I told them I don't go out to Mango Cove or Mango Beach. Never go over there. Too far. They didn't believe me."

A few hours later, back at the *Palmchat Gazette*, Beanie sat in the breakroom having his third cup of coffee of the day. At a table near the wall of ceiling-to-floor windows that allowed an abundance of sunshine to flood the large area with natural light, he was joined by his coworkers, Stevie Bishop and Caleb Olivier.

"I don't believe that fool, either," grumbled Caleb, the grumpy old journalist who'd worked at the paper for more than three decades. "He's not telling the truth."

"Unless maybe he is," countered Stevie, the slacker surfer dude whose family, the Bishops, were among the wealthiest on the island and in the world.

In the past, Beanie had found himself annoyed by Stevie's obtuseness, but after several years of working with the scion, he realized that Stevie possessed a savant-like approach to investigating. Initially, Stevie's theories seemed farfetched, but they were often spot on in the end. Additionally, Stevie had a hacker cousin, a mysterious family member whose identity, thus far, had remained anonymous. The hacker cousin had been instrumental in helping the *Palmchat Gazette* reporters obtain information the police wouldn't divulge.

"Well, I wouldn't expect you to be able to spot a liar if one bit you on the behind," said Caleb.

"Why would a liar bite me on the behind?" Stevie frowned. "And even if he did, wouldn't he just lie about it if I confronted him? A liar wouldn't tell me the truth. And that's how I would know that he was a liar."

Chuckling, Beanie said, "Which means that, actually, Stevie would be able to spot a liar if one bit him on the behind."

Caleb scowled. "Neither one of you idiots has the sense God gave a goat, and that's an insult to the goat."

Stevie frowned again. "Why is it an insult to the goat?"

"Let's get back to Mr. Iris," suggested Beanie, steering the conversation toward the original topic. "Is he a good suspect or not? Janvier likes him for the murder of Gavin de Grac, but you know I don't trust Janvier."

Caleb sighed. "I think I have to agree with Fields. Janvier might be right this time. Mr. Iris has motive, means, and opportunity."

Rubbing his chin, Beanie said, "Motive is the beef about the palm tree."

"Means is the gun," said Stevie. "The murder weapon belonged to Mr. Iris."

"And opportunity is Mr. Iris' lack of an alibi for the night de Grac was murdered," said Caleb. "Seashell Estates is not that far from Mango Beach. Only about thirty minutes. Iris had plenty of time to drive to Mango Beach, shoot de Grac, and drive home. You ask me, I'd say Mr. Iris is the killer."

Stevie nodded. "And don't forget the threatening text messages."

"Mr. Iris also went to prison for nearly beating one of his neighbors to death," said Beanie. "He's got a propensity to lash out and attack, but ..."

"But?" prompted Stevie.

"I don't know." Beanie finished his coffee, then sat the empty cup on the table. "Mr. Iris said Mr. de Grac took his gun from him."

Nostrils flared, Caleb frowned. "Don't tell me you believe that nonsense? That is the most fool explanation I ever heard!"

"But what if it's true?" suggested Stevie.

Shaking his head, Caleb said, "If you two don't stop talking foolishness, I'm going back to my desk. I have stories to write. I don't have time to entertain tomfoolery!"

Holding up a hand, Beanie said, "Look, I don't believe that de Grac took Mr. Iris' gun, but … hypothetically, let's say he did. If so, then … "

"Then Mr. de Grac was on Mango Beach near the sand dunes with Mr. Iris' gun," said Stevie.

Caleb said, "And then the question would be … why was de Grac on Mango Beach with a gun? In other words, why would he bring a gun to the beach?"

"And if he brought the gun to the beach," said Stevie. "Then how did he end up getting shot with it?"

"Well, if Mr. Iris told the truth," began Beanie, "then he didn't kill Mr. de Grac. And then the question would be, who did …?"

7

"I think I figured out why my mom has been so judgmental," said Noelle.

Sitting next to his wife on a bench beneath a palm tree, Beanie stared toward the playground. Ethan and a group of friends were playing a game that seemed to be a combination of hide and go seek and tag. Little Evan giggled and clapped his hands as he waddled around in the sandbox with several other toddlers, all of whom frolicked under the watchful eyes of three young moms.

After ending his day at the *Palmchat Gazette*, Beanie had texted his wife for an idea about dinner plans. She'd messaged back a reminder that she'd put goat cutlets in the crockpot that morning before leaving for work. In another hour or so, the meat would be ready. Tender and succulent, the cooked goat would be shredded. Noelle would finish the meat with a spicy guava jerk sauce to make goat sliders. She'd decided to take the boys to the neighborhood park because Ethan wouldn't stop inquiring about when the goat would be done.

"Why?" asked Beanie, though he wasn't sure he wanted to know. It was a lovely afternoon. Bright sun. Strong balmy breeze. The smells of jasmine, sea spray, and hibiscus mingled with the high-pitched squeals and whoops of childish delight and excitement. Beanie wanted to relax and soak up the lazy, carefree atmosphere. But, the slight hitch in his wife's voice hinted at a heavy heart.

Noelle exhaled and angled her body toward him. "A few weeks ago, mom made this comment …"

"Comment?" asked Beanie, smiling as Evan and his little pals shoveled sand into a bucket with earnest determination.

"We were laughing about Ethan being sly and sneaky," said Noelle. "I can't remember what he'd done."

"Something sly and sneaky?" guessed Beanie, glancing at his wife.

Noelle's eyes narrowed.

Beanie cleared his throat. "And then what happened?"

"And then mom said … " Noelle paused, rolling her eyes. "Your father was like that when he was a boy. Sly and sneaky. Ethan gets that from his grandfather."

Concerned and wary, Beanie turned toward his wife. "And what did you say?"

Shaking her head, Noelle said, "I sort of lost it. I told her, how could she think that? And how dare she say something so horrible? And things escalated until we were both screaming at each other. And then I left and …"

"And?"

Noelle frowned. "Ethan is not like my father. I mean, you don't think that, do you?"

Beanie glanced toward the playground. Ethan was still cutting up. Being playful and mischievous. Leading the other little boys around the playground, using the monkey bars, merry-go-round, and swings as an obstacle course.

"Roland …"

The sharp censure in Noelle's tone commanded Beanie's attention. Staring at her, he prayed for the right words to say and the phrases that would put her mind at ease. But, he could only be honest.

"Elle, I don't know your father," said Beanie. "You know I've never met him. You don't want me to meet—"

"But, you know what kind of person he is," said Noelle, her expression panicked, eyes intense. "You know that Ethan is nothing like him."

"Right," said Beanie, recalling what he knew about Noelle's father. "Ethan is not like your dad."

Josue Chartres, currently incarcerated, had been sentenced to spend the rest of his life in Tiverton, the maximum-security prison on a private island fifty miles from St. Killian. Once a cold-blooded enforcer for the PC-5, Chartres had assassinated those doomed to the cartel's dreaded Death List.

"Anyway, since that argument," said Noelle, "Mom has been sneaky and sly about pointing out my flaws and faults."

"Maybe Ethan is like his grandmother," suggested Beanie, trying for a bit of levity.

Noelle scowled. "That's not funny, Roland."

"I was just—"

"Mom got mad because I said I would never let the boys meet my father," said Noelle. "She said I was wrong for that. Cruel is actually the word she used. She accused me of being too hard on my father. Yes, he'd made mistakes, she said. And I was like, mistakes. I was like, Mom … Josue killed people."

"Murder is a bit more than a mistake."

"And then she tells me I'm not perfect," said Noelle, turning her body toward the playground, staring in that direction. "She tells me I've made mistakes. Bad choices and decisions ..."

Without warning, Detective Janvier's parting shot ricocheted through Beanie's mind. *She was innocent of that crime, yes, but certainly guilty of others, no?* The detective's words were buried in his subconscious but not deep enough to forget. He hated that Janvier's insinuation could catch him off guard. Force him to ruminate on doubts he shouldn't have.

"I told Mom that I don't care what she thinks," said Noelle. "Ethan and Evan will never have anything to do with their grandfather."

Ignoring his disturbing thoughts, Beanie said, "But they will find out about him, and I think they'll have questions."

Noelle sighed. "Maybe he'll be dead by then ... "

Beanie glanced at his wife. "Elle ..."

"I know that's a terrible thing to say," said Noelle, "but like you said, you don't know him ..."

"Still—"

"Trust me, Roland," said Noelle, staring at him. "That man does not deserve to know those sweet boys."

Concerned and confused by his wife's vehemence toward her father, which Beanie suspected had little to do with the man's past as a hitman, Beanie said, "Elle, why—"

"Mommy! Mommy!" Little Evan ran toward them on chubby little legs. "Push me on swing! Push me on swing, Mommy!"

"Okay, baby!" said Noelle, enveloping Evan into a fierce embrace. "Mommy will push you on the swing!"

As Noelle walked to the swings with little Evan, Beanie reflected on something else Janvier had said ...

Maybe you should ask your wife

Beanie didn't know if he wanted to ...

8

Beanie took a quick sip of his latte, purchased moments ago from the Hullabaloo Coffee Shop located in the Adagio Bay open-air mall. A popular tourist attraction, the sprawling shopping complex teemed with people at eleven o'clock in the morning.

Across from him at the small bistro table was Nora de Grac, the widow of Gavin de Grac.

A sales clerk at the mall's Chanel boutique, Nora was a well-put-together woman dressed to the nines in her Sunday best, an obvious job requirement considering the clientele of the high-end luxury store. Her hair was pulled back into a sculpted chignon, and she wore a pale green cardigan set over a black pencil skirt. Pearl earrings, a matching pearl necklace, and tasteful makeup completed her look.

After his interview with Mr. Iris the day before, and the subsequent speculation with his coworkers, Beanie decided a conversation with the victim's wife might provide additional information. Specifically, he wanted to find out if Mrs. de Grac believed Mr. Iris had murdered her husband or if she thought there might be a different suspect.

"Mrs. de Grac, thank you for agreeing to meet with me," started Beanie. He'd called the widow earlier that morning, around seven, when he arrived at the office. She'd been reluctant and aloof after he introduced himself and stated his business but eventually agreed to meet him before her shift at Chanel, which began at noon.

Her expression solemn and yet serene, Nora de Grac nodded. "You're welcome."

Beanie cleared his throat. "As I said on the phone, the police have identified a person of interest in your husband's murder."

Nora de Grac exhaled a shaky sigh. "Stanley Iris."

"Do you believe the police have the right suspect?"

"Stanley Iris is a horrible old man," said Nora, her speech slow and over-enunciated in that way some Palmchatters spoke when they wanted to under-emphasize their West Indian accent.

Probably another job requirement, Beanie figured.

"But to kill a man because of a palm tree is ridiculous and makes no sense," said Nora de Grac.

"Are you aware of the evidence against Mr. Iris?" asked Beanie, taking a sip of coffee.

"The detective told me that Stanley Iris' gun was used to kill Gav," said Nora de Grac. "And Iris left threatening messages on Gav's phone, which I knew about because Gav let me hear them."

Beanie said, "Mr. Iris claims that your husband took his gun during an argument they had a few weeks ago. Do you know if that's true or not?"

"I have no idea." Nora de Grac shook her head. "But ..."

"But?" asked Beanie.

Nora de Grac clasped her hands together and looked away as she wiped a tear from her cheek.

Beanie followed her gaze. Shoppers loitered in front of glass windows that showcased displays of everything from designer duds, kitschy tropical gifts, cosmetics, and souvenirs to shoes, diamonds, books, and musical instruments.

"Gav might have done something like that," said the widow. "Mr. Iris might be telling the truth about Gav taking his gun."

Taking a longer sip of coffee, Beanie said nothing, hoping his silence would compel her to continue.

Nora wiped another tear as her gaze dropped toward the table. "Gavin had hustler tendencies."

"What do you mean?"

"There's no telling what all he was into, or up to … " Nora glanced up at him. "I tried to stay out of it, and Gav always told me it was better for me not to know things, so … "

Beanie glanced at the clusters of mall patrons. Loaded with shopping bags, tourists in Palmchat Islands T-shirts strolled leisurely. Local Palmchatters strode at a brisk pace. He was curious about Gavin de Grac's hustler tendencies. The term hustler had many interpretations. A hustler could be a crafty, hard worker who made their own opportunities. Or, a hustler could be a sly manipulator who took advantage of others. Which interpretation might have defined Mr. de Grac?

Had the man been into something or up to something that could have gotten him killed?

"Gavin certainly was not perfect," said Nora, her voice shaky. "And he and I certainly didn't have a perfect relationship. Like most couples who've been together almost forever, we had our ups and downs. I walked out on him so many times, but I always came back …"

Beanie remained quiet as the widow removed a tissue from her purse and discreetly blew her nose.

"Gav was the love of my life," said Nora, her damp eyes vacant. "And now he's gone. And I'm alone."

"You didn't have children?"

"Not together." Nora shook her head. "I have two daughters from a previous relationship, but they both live in the States. Anyway … me and Gavin were supposed to spend the rest of our lives together, but that's not going to happen, and it's not Stanley Iris' fault."

"You seem sure about that," remarked Beanie.

"The man is crazy," said Nora. "But he's not a killer. There is something you might want to look into, though."

Beanie focused on the widow. "What's that?"

Nora opened her purse, slipped her hand inside, and removed an item. Seconds later, she placed the object on the table.

Frowning, Beanie stared at a hotel card key.

"I found it in Gav's things when I was looking for his favorite tie," explained Nora. "The one he'd told me he wanted to be buried in, which had belonged to his great-grandfather."

Picking up the key card, Beanie looked at the name and logo. Swaying Palms Inn. Beneath the name, a silhouette of two palm trees bending toward each other.

"There's a sticker on the back …"

Beanie flipped the key card. A round neon orange sticker near the corner of the card had the number 729 scrawled in black ink.

"That must be the room number, don't you think?"

Rubbing his jaw, Beanie said, "Maybe."

"I looked up the place online," said the widow. "Scuzzy, nasty low-rent motel in Little Turkey, of all places."

"Why would Mr. de Grac have a key to a room at the Swaying Palms Inn?" asked Beanie, more to himself than to the man's widow.

"Maybe it's got something to do with why Gavin was killed."

Beanie said nothing as he stared at the widow.

"Maybe you could find out," pleaded Nora.

Wary of making any promises, Beanie stayed noncommittal. "Maybe …"

"But if you can't figure out the business with the key," said Nora. "Then there's something else you could maybe check out … "

9

"I want you to listen to this message," said Nora, tapping the screen of her cellphone with her French-tipped, manicured index finger. "It came a week ago when Gav was out of town."

"Who is the message from?" asked Beanie.

Nora shrugged and held the phone out to him. "I have no idea."

Wary, Beanie took the phone and put it to his ear. After a few seconds of silence, a gruff, gravelly West Indian voice said, "Listen up, pretty lady. You tell your old man that Blitz is not playing about that money your old man owes him. You better tell him to settle up. He can't keep changing his number and avoiding calls forever. Nobody wants to hurt him, but it will be his fault if it comes to that …"

"Is that the only message you received from whoever that was?" asked Beanie, passing the cell phone back to Nora.

"So far, yes," said Nora, slipping the phone back into her purse.

"Did you tell Mr. de Grac?"

Nora shook her head. "I didn't get a chance to. As soon as he got back to St. Killian, he got very busy with some new business deals that he couldn't tell me about because they were confidential, he claimed, and then I took on a few extra shifts at the store. We kept missing each other all week and then …"

As Nora's eyes welled with tears, Beanie understood why she'd trailed off. "You have any idea who Blitz is? You know anything about the money Mr. de Grac owed Blitz?"

"Blitz is Gav's bookie," said Nora. "Gav liked to gamble. He played the lottery a lot. Went to the casinos. Bet on goat races. Gav got in trouble for not paying gambling debts before. Got beat up pretty bad. Blitz did it. He came to our house. He hit me, too. Threw me against the wall. Blitz told Gav he would kill him if he didn't pay up. Gav told me that Blitz was not bluffing. Gav said Blitz had killed guys before. So, I took a few extra shifts to help him settle the debt. Anyway, I was thinking …"

"What?"

Nora leaned forward. Voice lowered, she said, "What if Gav got killed because he couldn't pay a gambling debt? What if Blitz made good on his threat to kill him?"

Beanie exhaled. He supposed it was possible but not likely. Bookies wanted to get paid. Dead men could not settle debts. And lifeless bodies were a hassle.

"Did you tell the police about the message?"

"The detective blew me off," said Nora. "He wouldn't even listen to the message. He told me he had the killer. Stanley Iris. The detective told me to go home and mourn my husband and leave the police work to the professionals. But I was thinking … hoping actually …"

Not surprised by Janvier's dismissiveness, Beanie asked, "Hoping what?"

Nora de Grac took a deep breath. "The police are looking at the wrong suspect. They need to investigate Blitz. The cops won't listen to me, but maybe you could tell the police that Gav might have been killed because of his gambling debts."

Beanie said, "Mrs. de Grac, I'm pretty sure Detective Janvier won't listen to me. He and I don't have the best relationship. He's going to tell me to stay out of the investigation."

"Well, then, maybe you could look into the gambling debts," suggested Nora, her pale brown eyes intense and imploring. "Maybe you could find out if Blitz had anything to do with Gavin's death."

"I don't know— "

"Please ..." begged Nora, not bothering to wipe the tears away. "Can you just try to see if you can find out anything? I know the police believe Stanley Iris killed Gav, but what if he didn't? I really hate the thought of Gav's killer getting away with murder ..."

10

The Swaying Palms Inn was just as Nora de Grac had described it, thought Beanie.

Scuzzy and low-rent, which wasn't surprising, considering the neighborhood.

Located west of the St. Killian Airport, Little Turkey was comprised of hardworking lower-class Palmchatters. Most Little Turkey residents were descendants of Turkish immigrants who'd come to the island centuries ago to work at a local sugar mill.

The wealthy sugar baron who founded the Palmchat Sugar Company provided housing, hospitals, and schools for his employees and their families. But after the mill closed, the neighborhood experienced a rapid economic decline, leading to the crumbling disrepair of Little Turkey's infrastructure and essential services.

After enduring decades of impoverished conditions, the proud, strong-willed Little Turkey residents had become known for staging protests when they felt they were being marginalized or ignored. As Beanie drove through the neighborhood, he was thankful the palm-lined streets weren't teeming with people, demanding better roads or schools or more police presence.

After his interview with Gavin de Grac's widow, Nora, Beanie stopped at Pourciau Square for an early lunch from his favorite food truck, the Loco Goat. Eating his goat stew, mango rice, and stewed plantains at one of the wooden tables in the square's dining area, Beanie reflected on Nora's suggestion that he investigate room 729 at the Swaying Palms Inn.

Beanie suspected the widow believed her husband had been engaged in some sort of indiscretion, possibly with another woman. He figured she wanted an accounting of Gavin's final days. More than likely, if de Grac had been having an affair and some evidence of his infidelity still existed at the motel, Nora was hoping to discover the other woman's identity. Beanie didn't want to get into the middle of a woman-scorned plot. However, it was possible that de Grac had used the motel for one of his hustles. Perhaps some quasi-criminal shenanigans might have gotten him killed. For that reason, Beanie wanted to check out the motel.

Mr. Iris seemed to be the guilty party; however, Beanie wanted to explore all possibilities.

Beanie drove his SUV across the cracked concrete parking lot and pulled into an empty slot about ten feet away from room 729, which was at the opposite end of the reception office, near the property entrance. Shifting into park, Beanie cut the engine. He pulled the card key from his pocket and exited the vehicle. Wishing he had his sunglasses, Beanie used his hand to shade his eyes from the harsh, bright noonday sun as he walked to the motel room.

The L-shaped lodging, constructed of stucco with a sun-faded, red-tiled roof, had probably never seen better days. Beanie imagined it had been built for extreme budget travelers. Tourists who cared little for luxury, comfort, or a glamorous location. Vacationers who only needed a place to shower and sleep.

Staring at room number 729, Beanie took in the peeling fuchsia-colored paint. Rust stains trailed in snaking lines along the stucco bordering the door. A rectangular, six-paned window was practically opaque from the build-up of dust, grime, and water spots.

Reaching into his pocket, he pulled out the card key Nora had given him.

Did the thing even still work? Beanie took a deep breath. Well, it would, or it wouldn't. Beanie pressed the card against the key reader. Seconds later, a small green light beeped. There was a faint click. Beanie pushed the knob down and opened the door.

Beanie walked into the room.

The sharp scent of bleach and lemon cleaner hit him in the face, spiraling into his nose, causing his nostrils to flare. Coughing, Beanie closed the door behind him and looked around. The room was basic. Nondescript island décor. Two twin beds plus a rollaway bed. Three occupants, maybe, thought Beanie. Interesting. Why would Gavin be in a motel room with two extra beds? Perhaps he hadn't used the room for an illicit affair. Two particle board night tables with lamps on each of them. A small chair in one corner. A window AC unit beneath the window opposite the door. A medium-sized dresser across from the bed with a small television on top of it. A door near the chair opened into a tiny bathroom.

Beanie sighed. He was no longer sure about his decision to investigate the motel room. What did he expect to find? Judging from the smell of cleaning agents, housekeeping had already tidied the room. Whatever evidence he might have found was probably gone. Wiped away. Tossed into the trash. Still, he figured he might as well take a look around. Then he could call Nora and tell her the motel room had been a bust.

Fifteen minutes later, Beanie realized he might have been wrong about the motel room.

He'd found something.

He just wasn't sure what it was …

Leaving the motel room, Beanie secured what he'd found in his SUV and then walked toward the small portico where the reception office was located. Inside, the air was stuffy despite the A/C unit humming in the window.

"Can I help you?"

After introducing himself, Beanie said, "I'm working on a story about a man named Gavin de Grac. He was found dead on Mango Beach."

The motel clerk frowned and shook his head. "I don't know anything about a dead man on the beach."

"No, I understand," said Beanie, careful not to alarm the clerk. "But, I believe Mr. de Grac may have stayed in one of your rooms. Number 729."

"I don't know anything about anybody who stays at this motel," said the clerk. "I check people in, but I don't really pay attention to nobody. I'm not one for getting into peoples' business."

"So if I showed you a photo of Mr. de Grac," said Beanie, "you wouldn't be able to tell me if you saw him around or—"

"Nope." The clerk shook his head. "I actually try not to notice people. Place like this, you get people doing all kinds of things they probably shouldn't be doing. I don't want nobody thinking I saw something I shouldn't."

Beanie nodded. "I understand."

"Who you need to talk to is Ferris," said the clerk.

Beanie frowned. "Ferris?"

"He works here on the weekends," said the clerk. "Ferris gets into everybody's business."

"Is that right?" asked Beanie.

"That's because he don't have no business of his own," said the clerk, chuckling slightly. "No wife. No kids. No life. I'm sure he seen whoever was in 729."

"And he'll be here this weekend?" asked Beanie.

"Well, he would, but he had to take some days off," said the clerk. "Went to Jamaica to see his mama. She fell and broke her hip."

"When will he be back?"

"Maybe in a few weeks," said the clerk. "I'm not sure."

Reaching into his pocket, Beanie took out his wallet, opened it, and removed a business card. "When Ferris comes back, could you tell him to call me?"

11

"Where did you find this?" asked Stevie Bishop, sitting across from Beanie, his elbows propped on the table.

"At the Swaying Palms Inn," answered Beanie, taking a sip of coffee. "In room 729."

"Where specifically in the motel room?" asked Caleb, seated to the right of Beanie, sipping an afternoon cup of green tea.

"In the bottom drawer of one of the nightstands," said Beanie, recalling the discovery. After checking the dresser drawers, and the nightstand drawers on the left side of the bed, he'd found them empty. Beanie had expected the nightstand on the right side of the bed would have nothing in it, either.

He'd been wrong.

In the bottom drawer, he'd discovered a manila file folder.

Inside were several 5x7 photos and a business card secured with a large paper clip.

"Wonder who this guy is?" asked Stevie, shuffling through the photos.

Beanie had studied the pictures in the motel room.

All of the photos had the same subject. A man Beanie surmised to be in his late fifties, maybe early sixties. He looked like an old surfer dude with tanned leathery skin. Crow's feet and deep lines marked his forehead, gaunt cheeks, and chin. His thick, scraggly sun-bleached hair was gray with blonde highlights.

In most of the photos, a few of which appeared to have been taken with a close-up telephoto lens, he wore wrinkled khaki shorts, a short-sleeved Hawaiian shirt, and leather sandals. Beanie thought he looked like one of those former business executives who, fed up with the corporate grind, escaped to the islands, eager to live a carefree life of no shoes, no shirt, and no reason to shower each morning.

Whoever had photographed him seemed to have done so without his knowledge. He'd been captured engaged in daily life. Riding a bike. Walking out of a grocery store. Having a drink at a bar. Appearing to give a group of tourists directions. Eating jerk goat at a roadside stand. Laughing with a woman hawking wares at an open-air flea market near the marina.

"What about this?" asked Stevie, holding what looked to Beanie like a store receipt.

"What's that?" asked Caleb.

"Receipt from Palm-Mart," said Stevie. "Somebody bought a bunch of junk. Candy. Soda. Chips."

"Where did you find that?" Beanie asked, reaching for the receipt. Something was written on the back. He flipped it over. 4477 Vane Avenue. "I know this street. Vane Avenue. It's in Handweg."

"The receipt fell from between two of the photos," said Stevie.

"Wonder if it has anything to do with Gavin de Grac," mused Beanie, staring at the items printed on the Palm-Mart receipt. "Or maybe the guy in the photos."

"That receipt probably don't have nothing to do with anything," said Caleb. "Just like the man in the photos. He probably doesn't have anything to do with Gavin de Grac, either."

"But I think he does," said Beanie. "Because the card key still worked. Makes me think de Grac was still renting that motel room."

Stevie nodded. "If de Grac had already checked out, the key card would have been deactivated."

"Right," said Beanie. "So, now the question is, did de Grac put this manila folder in the nightstand drawer. If so, why? And did de Grac take the pictures? If not, why would he want photos of this man?"

Stevie said, "It all comes back to this question—who's the guy in the photos? If you can identify him, then that might shed some light onto whatever connection he might have had with Gavin de Grac."

"Maybe this man knows the guy in the photos," suggested Caleb, tapping the business card lying on top of the manila file.

Beanie glanced at the name on the card: RUBEN FITZGERALD, PRIVATE INVESTIGATOR/HOSTEL OWNER

"I know that guy," said Stevie, placing the photos on the table in a neat stack.

"What guy?" asked Caleb.

"The private eye," said Stevie.

Beanie glanced at him. "You know Ruben Fitzgerald."

Nodding, Stevie explained that he and Vivian had talked to the private investigator for a story about a woman who'd been poisoned at St. Killian General Hospital.

"You think he'll talk to me?" asked Beanie.

"Yeah," said Stevie, leaning back in his chair. "But only if you pay him."

Caleb harrumphed and waved a hand dismissively. "Oh, he's one of those?"

"Cost me a couple of hundred bucks for the information he had," said Stevie.

"Well, that's not in my budget at the moment," said Beanie, standing. "Think I'll try the guy who left the threatening message on Nora de Grac's phone instead."

Back at his desk, Beanie consulted his notes and located the number of the person who'd threatened Nora de Grac. The manila file filled with photos of the mystery guy no longer intrigued him. He was more inclined to investigate the threatening caller. Nora believed the man who'd left the messages might have been Gavin's bookie. If Gavin hadn't paid his debts, the bookie would have sent someone to collect. The debt collector might have shot Gavin.

Not because the bookie wanted Gavin dead, however.

Beanie imagined that Gavin's death might have been an accident. Maybe the debt collector confronted Gavin. Used the gun to scare him. But the murder weapon belonged to Stanley Iris. So, how would the debt collector have gotten Iris' gun? Beanie pressed his thumb against the spot between his eyebrows.

If Stanley Iris was telling the truth about de Grac taking his gun, then possibly, when the debt collector confronted Gavin, the man pulled the pistol on the debt collector. Maybe Gavin and the debt collector wrestled for the weapon. In the struggle, the debt collector could have gotten the gun and shot de Grac.

Beanie picked up the receiver from his desk phone and dialed the threatening caller's number.

"What?" barked the person who answered.

Clearing his throat, Beanie said, "I'm calling about a message you left …"

"Message I left for who?"

"A woman named Nora de Grac," said Beanie. "You wanted her to call you about—"

"She got the money her old man owes?"

"Well, actually, I don't know if you heard," began Beanie, grabbing a pen from the pencil holder next to his computer, "but Nora's old man, Gavin, passed away, so—"

"Gavin is dead?"

Picking up on the shock in the man's stern tone, Beanie asked, "So you didn't know?"

"What happened to him?" asked the man. "Accident? Heart attack?"

Beanie twirled the pen slowly between his fingers. If the guy didn't know how Gavin de Grac died, then Beanie figured maybe he wasn't talking to de Grac's killer.

"He was shot to death."

"Figures," scoffed the man.

"You have any idea who might have killed him?"

"Who are you?" asked the man. "Why you want to know who killed de Grac?"

"My name is Roland Bean," said Beanie. "I'm a reporter for the *Palmchat Gazette*, and I'm covering the story of Mr. de Grac's murder."

"Well, I don't know who killed him," the man said. "And I don't really care. All I know is somebody better come up with that money he owed. Or else …"

12

Beanie had just taken a second sip of his first cup of coffee that morning when his desk phone buzzed.

He jabbed an index finger at the speaker button. "Roland Bean."

"Hey, it's Millie," said the paper's front desk receptionist. "You have a visitor."

"A visitor?" echoed Beanie, frowning as he grabbed his mouse and checked his calendar. He didn't recall a meeting with anyone. His schedule was clear.

"Guy says his name is Zach Preston," said Millie. "Says he has information about the Gavin de Grac murder."

"Zach Preston …" Beanie repeated. He leaned back in his chair. The name wasn't familiar, but if the man knew something about the de Grac case, Beanie wanted to talk to him.

Three days had passed since he'd gotten any new details about de Grac's death. According to Fields, the police still liked Stanley Iris as the murderer but had yet to formally charge the man. The clues given to him by Nora de Grac hadn't panned out. Though Beanie had spoken to the man who'd threatened Nora, the guy had refused to give Beanie his name. And as for the photos in the manila file, Beanie had phoned Ruben Fitzgerald, but the private investigator had yet to return his call.

"Can you take Mr. Preston to the conference room?" asked Beanie. "I'll meet him in there."

Moments later, Beanie walked into the large, spacious room. Bright early morning sunshine streamed through the wall of windows, casting a golden glow across the man sitting at the table, sitting ramrod straight.

A man Beanie recognized immediately.

Zach Preston was the man in the photos Beanie had found in the manila file in room 729 at the Swaying Palms Inn in Little Turkey. Confusion rocked him. And yet, the man's presence at the table was confirmation of a suspicion Beanie harbored—there was a definite connection between Gavin de Grac and Zach Preston.

Walking to the chair directly across from the man, Beanie took a seat. "Good morning, Mr. Preston. How are you?"

Preston gave a solemn nod.

"Do you want any coffee?" asked Beanie. "Water?"

"All I want, young man, is to tell you the truth about what happened to Gavin de Grac," said Preston, his brown-eyed stare penetrating.

"Okay …" said Beanie, reaching into the pocket of his Dockers to remove his phone, which he placed on the table. "Do you mind if I record you?"

"I do not," said Preston. "I actually prefer it as I do not want anything I say misconstrued or taken out of context."

"Right," said Beanie, giving the man what he hoped was a reassuring smile, though he was wary. Zach Preston appeared as though he was struggling to contain himself. Like he might explode at any minute, for any reason. As such, Beanie cautioned himself not to make any sudden moves.

After clearing his throat, Beanie activated the recording app. "Mr. Preston, please tell me your full name and the spelling—"

"My name doesn't matter," said Preston. "What matters is the police are looking at the wrong man. I read your story. It said the cops are looking at a man named Stanley Iris as the killer, but Iris didn't shoot Gavin."

"How do you know that Stanley Iris didn't shoot Gavin de Grac?"

Zach Preston held up a hand. "I'll get to that, but first …"

"First?" prompted Beanie.

"You need to know that Gavin de Grac was a good man," said Preston. "Don't let anybody tell you different. And I know you probably heard some bad things about him. He wasn't perfect, but who is? None of us can cast the first stone."

Beanie shifted in his chair. How long would Preston take to get to the point? With his tremulous, grave baritone, he sounded like he was giving a eulogy. Beanie wanted the man to cut to the chase, but he understood that people with information could be stingy about sharing it. Sometimes, they enjoyed a captive audience and wanted to divulge their knowledge bit by bit.

"Gavin was also a good friend of mine," said Preston. "He didn't deserve what happened to him. He was betrayed because he did the right thing."

"What do you mean?" asked Beanie.

Preston exhaled. "Gavin de Grac was killed because he was trying to make sure I stayed alive."

Beanie shook his head. "I don't understand."

Scowling, Preston said, "A few weeks ago, three men came here to kill me."

"Why?" asked Beanie. He was becoming increasingly doubtful that Zach Preston had any viable details about de Grac's murder. He had a feeling this meeting would be a waste of time. Preston might be a lonely old coot seeking attention. It wasn't uncommon for people to pretend to have crucial information about murder cases. They often obstructed justice, providing false leads because they wanted to feel helpful and important.

"I don't really want to get into why they wanted me dead," said Preston.

Beanie told himself not to roll his eyes.

"What matters is that Gavin warned me about their plans to take me out," said Preston. "And that is why Gavin is dead."

Rubbing his jaw, Beanie said, "So … these three men killed Gavin?"

Preston shook his head. "Only one of them killed him. The other two are innocent."

"What's the guilty man's name?"

"I don't know …"

Tempering his frustration, Beanie asked, "Well, do you know what the man looks like? Or—"

"No, what I meant to say was, I don't know which man is guilty," said Preston. "I know the three men who came to kill me. I can give you their names. I just don't know which of the three killed Gavin. That's what you need to find out."

"Mr. Preston, I think you should take this information to the police," said Beanie.

"I don't trust cops."

"Why not?"

"I just don't," said Preston, his gaze drifting.

"Something tells me that you don't want to have to tell the cops why three men wanted you dead," guessed Beanie.

Preston's eyes narrowed. "I came to you because I want justice. Because I don't want an innocent man to go to jail while a guilty man goes free."

"Because if the guilty man goes free, then he can come after you again?"

The tight lines around Preston's mouth relaxed a bit. "I believe this man intends to see me dead. I would like him locked up before he has a chance to put me in the dirt …"

13

As the nine o'clock morning ferry from St. Killian to St. Xavier sailed over slightly chopping waters, Beanie stared at his cell phone. The file opened on his notetaking app showed the three names he'd typed two days ago during the weird meeting with Zach Preston.

Dennis Woodard, Archibald "Archie" Hall, and Tarragon Ungaro.

Beanie hoped to talk to all three of the men today. It was Saturday. His weekends were usually reserved for family, but from time to time, work intruded.

Beanie closed the app, put his phone back into the pocket of his trousers, and glanced out at the dark aqua waters of the Caribbean. Trying not to feel like a complete fool, he reminded himself that every lead had to be vetted and that most leads led to nowhere. How many times had Officer Fields complained to him about calling a list of witnesses who hadn't heard anything or seen anything and didn't want to get involved? Following up on information was part of the job.

Nevertheless, Beanie was still uncertain about Zach Preston.

The man's story was vague and bizarre. Preston's insistence on remaining obtuse and secretive about crucial details bothered Beanie.

His suspicions increased as Preston refused to answer his questions. Preston didn't want to tell him why the three men wanted him dead. Didn't want to talk about how he knew the men. Didn't want to reveal how he knew Gavin de Grac. As for how Gavin had discovered the men's plans, Preston claimed not to know and insisted it didn't matter. He wouldn't tell Beanie how Gavin knew the men. Wouldn't say anything about Gavin's warning that he was a target.

All that mattered, according to Preston, was figuring out which of the three men had killed Gavin de Grac.

Dennis Woodard, Archibald "Archie" Hall, or Tarragon Ungaro.

Following a search of several different personal data research databases, Beanie gathered enough information on the men to create dossiers.

Dennis Woodard, a 61-year-old, had been born in the Bahamas but moved to the Palmchat Islands when he was eight. He'd never married and currently worked at the St. Xavier Post Office as a mail carrier. Additional employment records showed Woodard had been fired from his job at a small bank, where he'd worked as a teller. Beanie couldn't find a reason for the termination. He thought maybe Woodard tried to rob the place, but the man had no criminal history.

Tarragon Ungaro was sixty-five and unemployed but possessed a permit to sell fish, game, and produce at farmer's markets. He was divorced and had one son. The criminal databases showed several arrests for drunk and disorderly conduct, battery, assault, and one attempted murder charge, which had been dropped due to lack of evidence.

Archibald "Archie" Hall, a 62-year-old grocery store janitor, was married, had four children, and nine grandkids. Hall had no criminal history, but Beanie found a civil complaint filed against Hall. Apparently, the old man had foiled a robbery at a gas station convenience store. The thief sued Hall for pain and suffering, claiming Hall had body-slammed him after spying the robber slip a pack of gum into his back pocket.

What Beanie hadn't uncovered was any connection between Preston and the three men. His check into Preston's background revealed the man to be an ex-pat who'd arrived on the islands twelve years prior. Originally from Boston, Massachusetts, he'd moved to St. Killian and lived a transient lifestyle, residing in several different neighborhoods and working the occasional odd job.

Crazy thing was that Beanie hadn't been able to find any other information about Zach Preston beyond the man's first two years on the island. The ten years following were a mystery. Beanie could find no trace of the man. He'd searched criminal records, public service databases, school records, and employment databases but came up empty. Zach Preston seemed to have disappeared for ten years before he showed up in the *Palmchat Gazette* conference room.

After disembarking in St. Xavier, the capital of the Palmchat Islands, where the men resided, Beanie hailed a cab and gave the driver the address of Archie Hall.

Beanie's grandparents had been from St. X, as the capital was colloquially known, but he'd only visited a handful of times. He wasn't familiar with the different areas but knew most locations were referred to in terms of their direction from the capital buildings in the center of town. The island, shaped like a five-armed starfish, was on the smaller side. Each arm had a unique climate, landscape, and socioeconomic bracket.

Tomato Shores, where Archie Hall lived, was a neighborhood southeast of the capital, on what St. X residents called the Third Arm. Though somewhat economically depressed, the area thrived with locally owned businesses, including several grocery stores, tourist shops, and a small bank. From the backseat of the cab, gazing out of the window, Beanie noticed a large medical clinic, a law office, and an insurance company. Through the maze of narrow streets, colorful chattel houses dotted the landscape.

"Here you are," announced the driver, pulling along the curb in front of a small house painted pale lavender with yellow trim.

"How much do I owe you?" asked Beanie, removing his wallet from the back pocket of his jeans.

"You going to need a ride back to the ferry after your visit?" asked the driver.

Beanie chuckled. "Actually, I'm going to need a ride to two more places before I can head back to the ferry."

"Well, I can wait for you," said the driver. "Take you to those other places you need to go and then back to the ferry."

Catching the driver's gaze in the rearview mirror, Beanie could see the eagerness in the man's dark eyes.

"I'm not sure how long I'll be," said Beanie, though he doubted his conversations with the men would take very long.

The driver shrugged. "Saturdays are slow."

Beanie rubbed his jaw. The driver would probably pad his price a bit, but for the convenience of not having to figure out the logistics of traveling in St. X, he figured it was worth the extra cash.

"And how much would that be?"

The driver quoted a price. As Beanie suspected, the man had added a convenience surcharge, but the fee for having a private driver wasn't excessive.

Moments later, Beanie knocked on the frame of a screen door.

After a minute or so, during which Beanie knocked again, the exterior door opened. A petite island woman, possibly in her mid-forties, wearing a St. Xavier Postal Office uniform, gave him a skeptical glare. "Can I help you?"

"I hope so," said Beanie. "I'm looking for Archie Hall."

The woman's skepticism turned to outright suspicion. "And who are you?"

"My name is Roland Bean. I'm a reporter for the *Palmchat Gazette*," said Beanie, handing the woman a business card.

After a pause, she opened the screen door enough to slip an arm through the crack and snatch the card from him. Pulling the screen door closed, she secured the latch and stared at the card.

A moment later, she looked up at him. "What is this about?"

"I want to talk to Mr. Hall about a story I'm working on."

"A story?"

"A news article," said Beanie, realizing that being vague would get him nowhere with this woman. Forget playing his cards close to the vest. He had to lay them all on the table, or she was liable to slam the door in his face.

The woman frowned.

Clearing his throat, Beanie said, "A few days ago, in St. Killian, where I'm from, a man was found murdered on the beach. The dead man's name was Gavin de Grac. Recently, I received information that leads me to believe that Mr. Hall might have known the victim. I'd like to ask Mr. Hall if he has any idea about who might have wanted to kill Gavin de Grac."

The woman shook her head. "Arch doesn't know nobody that would kill people. I don't know where you got your information, mister, but they told you wrong."

Suppressing an exhale, Beanie asked, "Is Mr. Hall here?"

"He's at work," said the woman. "He's got a double shift today."

Recalling that Archie Hall was a grocery store janitor, Beanie said, "Okay, well ... would you mind giving him my card and telling him to give me a call."

"I'll tell him you came by," said the woman before she slammed the door in his face.

Hearing the deadbolt tumble into the locked position, Beanie sighed. He wasn't surprised by the woman's doubt. He sounded like a crazy person. How could she know he was telling the truth? Anyone could print a business card. And his story came across as suspicious. A man was found dead in St. Killian. Archie might have known him and might know who killed him. But what else could he have said? A suspicious old surfer dude told me Archie is part of a trio who traveled to St. Killian to kill him and might be the man who killed Gavin de Grac?

Zach Preston's claims were outlandish. They didn't deserve to be taken seriously, let alone repeated. Beanie couldn't believe he was going to waste his Saturday harassing three old guys who probably had nothing to do with Gavin de Grac's murder.

Walking down the concrete path away from the porch, Beanie wanted to return to the dock, get on a ferry, and head back to St. Killian.

Instead, he got back into the cab and gave the driver the next address.

14

Tarragon Ungaro lived in Conch Shell Forest, another Third Arm enclave of lower-middle-class citizens.

Beanie found the man on his porch, sitting on a stool that struggled to support his massive girth, which quivered and undulated beneath a thin, sweat-stained Aerie Islands Starfish cricket T-shirt. With a large knife, he cleaned the fish. A large dog slept beneath the stool where he sat. Beanie forced himself to push away a mental image of the obese man smushing the dog after the stool collapsed under his weight.

"Excuse me, sir, I'm looking for Tarragon Ungaro."

Scraping fish scales into a cardboard box, the man didn't look up but said, "That's me."

"Excuse me for showing up unannounced," said Beanie. "I don't mean to take up too much of your time, but—"

"Get to it, son," instructed the man.

"Right." Beanie cleared his throat. "Do you know the name Gavin de Grac?"

"Should I ...?"

Beanie pinched the bridge of his nose as he stared at the translucent fish scales falling into the box. "Gavin de Grac is dead. He was shot to death. His body was found on a beach in St. Killian."

"St. Killian?"

"Have you been there recently?" asked Beanie, trying to ignore the pungent stench of sweat and dead fish.

The man shook his head. "Had a sister used to lived there, but she moved to Jamaica three years ago. Haven't been to St. Killian since then. No reason to go."

Beanie sighed.

The man stopped scraping the fish and glanced at him with curious green eyes. "Why you asking me about a man who died on the beach in St. Killian?"

Beanie wanted to shrug and confess that he had no earthly idea, but he said, "I was told you might know the victim, but—"

"Who told you that?"

"You know a man named Zach Preston?"

The man frowned. "I know some Prestons. They stay in Fourth Arm. But I don't know a Zach Preston. Least, I don't think I do. Maybe he came into the shop one day. I fix cars."

Beanie recalled from his research of Tarragon Ungaro that the man was a mechanic and worked at a local shop.

"And he told you I know that dead man in St. Killian?" asked Tarragon. "Zach Preston said that about me? Did he tell you where he knows me from?"

"Not exactly," said Beanie, deciding not to tell the man about Zach's claims that Tarragon, along with Archie and Bennie, had come to St. Killian to kill him. "Listen, Mr. Ungaro. I'm sorry I bothered you. I think I've gotten some bad information."

Tarragon resumed scraping his fish. "I reckon you did …"

15

"Last stop …" announced Beanie, rattling off the address of Dennis Woodard, who lived in Blossom Beach, a solidly middle-class neighborhood located in the Second Arm.

Beanie figured he might as well go for the trifecta.

Woodard was outside watering his lawn, which was small but well-tended, with fruit trees and a row of vibrant orange hibiscus bushes in front of the porch.

Beanie approached the man, preparing for scowls and suspicion. "Excuse me, sir?"

The man looked up. "Yes?" His face was expressionless, but his eyes held a hint of inquisitive merriment.

Beanie introduced himself as an investigative reporter from the *Palmchat Gazette.* The man smiled, then proceeded to tell Beanie how he'd taught his children to read using the award-winning newspaper.

"My wife didn't like it because, at the time, what was in the papers was mostly about The Fury," said Woodard. "She didn't want them reading about death and cannibalism, but they weren't scared or anything."

Beanie nodded at the man's unusual approach. He could imagine

Noelle losing her mind if he suggested reading their boys real-life horror stories about a heinous serial killer.

"They liked the stories. They were fascinated, and they wanted to keep reading, and that's how they learned. When you want to teach a person something, you have to find a way to make it interesting and engaging."

"That's true," agreed Beanie.

"And the articles were very well written," said the man. "I forget the writer … "

"Caleb Olivier, most likely," supplied Beanie.

The man's face lit up. "Yes! That's right. Caleb Olivier. Is he still working at the paper?"

"He is," said Beanie and refrained from telling Mr. Woodard that Caleb hardly worked and now spent most of his time complaining, grumbling, and getting facts wrong.

"Please tell him how much I enjoyed his stories."

"I will," Beanie promised. "Mr. Woodard, the reason I stopped by is because I wanted to ask you about a man named Gavin de Grac. Do you know him?"

"Gavin de Grac." Woodard closed his eyes for a moment, then opened them, tilted his head back as though the answer might be in the clouds, and then stared at Beanie. Shaking his head, Woodard said, "I don't think I do, and I am sure I'd remember. De Grac is an unusual name. Why do you ask?"

Beanie gave Woodard the same explanation he'd given Tarragon Ungaro and Archie Hall's wife. A man named Zach Preston claimed that Woodard might know something about the murder of Gavin de Grac, a St. Killian resident found shot to death on Mango Beach.

"I don't know nobody who lives in St. Killian," said Woodard. "I've never been there. I don't know anything about a dead man found on a beach."

"Well, I didn't think you—"

"How did he die?" asked Woodard.

"Shot to death."

With pursed lips, the man shook his head. "Shame. And you trying to solve the crime? Trying to figure out who shot him?"

"Something like that," said Beanie. Again, he had no interest in telling Woodard that he was trying to figure out if *he* had killed Gavin de Grac. "Anyway—"

"So the police don't have no idea who killed the man?"

"They have a suspect," said Beanie. "But they haven't arrested him yet."

"Why not?" asked Woodard. "If they think he killed the man, seems to me they ought to arrest the suspect, don't you think? Get a dangerous criminal off the street before he kills again."

"Yeah, you would think that, but …" Trailing off, Beanie glanced toward the cab, parked on the curb in front of the house, waiting for him. He was more than ready to head back to the ferry.

"Who is the suspect?"

Beanie glanced back at Woodard. "What? Oh. Um, he's a local St. Killian man. The dead man's neighbor."

"And the police think this neighbor killed the dead man?"

Nodding, Beanie said, "There is evidence connecting him to the crime."

"What evidence?"

Beanie frowned at the man, who seemed more interested in watering the hibiscus bushes, but there was a prurient curiosity in the man's voice. Beanie pegged him as a bored busybody.

"The victim was killed with his neighbor's gun. The neighbor threatened him. The victim and the neighbor had beef, and the neighbor doesn't have an alibi for the night of the murder."

Bennie Woodward looked at him with wide eyes. "I don't know what the cops are waiting for. Seems like enough evidence to arrest the neighbor, you ask me."

"Yeah, I agree," said Beanie.

"But the man you told me about … Preston … he doesn't think the neighbor killed the man," said Woodard.

Beanie shook his head. "No, he doesn't."

"He thinks I know who killed the man," said Woodard, training the water hose on a different section of the bushes.

"But you don't."

"I would tell you and the police if I did," said Woodard. "I don't know Gavin de Grac. Or this man Preston. But I want to know."

Beanie was confused. "You want to know what?"

"I want to know why that man, Preston, thinks I know who killed de Grac," said Woodard. "I'd like to have a conversation with Preston. So, if he calls you again, I want you to give him my contact information."

16

"Daddy!" Ethan shouted. "Daddy!"

Startled slightly, Beanie turned from the kitchen counter, where he and Noelle were dicing mangoes and peppers for the goat stew and rice they planned to make for dinner.

"What is it, buddy?" asked Beanie, laying the knife down.

With a furious grimace, Ethan said, "Evan won't give me the blue crayon."

"Blue crayon," mimicked little Evan, moving his hand back and forth across the coloring book, creating what appeared to be rows and rows of blue smears. "Blue crayon."

"Because Evan is using it," said Beanie, walking to the kitchen table where the boys sat across from each other. A stack of coloring books and a box of crayons served as a makeshift centerpiece. "When he's finished, you can use it."

"But he's never going to finish, Daddy!" Ethan complained. "He's been using it too long! I have to color the ocean blue, Daddy! Evan is not drawing the ocean or the sky. Make him give it to me, Daddy."

"Ocean blue sky!" Evan laughed, continuing to color outside the lines of the picture in the coloring book, which was of a smiling cartoon dog. "Sky blue ocean!"

Exhaling, Beanie held out his hand toward his youngest son. "Evan, give Daddy the blue crayon."

Evan looked up at him and frowned. "No, Daddy! I need blue crayon."

Worried by the fierce tremor in Evan's voice, Beanie said, "Daddy will give the blue crayon back to you, okay? Just let me see it."

Eyes narrowed, Evan gave him an uncertain, suspicious scowl, but he handed over the blue crayon.

Holding the coveted crayon with both hands, Beanie snapped it in half.

"Daddy!" Ethan gasped, his eyes gleaming with delight and mischief. "You broke the crayon!"

"Daddy break crayon," said Evan, clapping his hands. "Daddy break crayon!"

Smiling at his little tykes, Beanie handed one half of the blue crayon to Ethan and the other half to Evan.

"Now you both have a blue crayon," said Beanie.

As the boys cheered, Beanie shook his head, thankful to have avoided what was sure to escalate into a crisis.

Turning from the boys, happily working on their respective drawings, Beanie stopped dead in his tracks.

Arms folded, Noelle glared at him.

Now what? Beanie thought, staring at his wife.

"Did you really just break the crayon in half?"

Walking back to the counter, Beanie picked up the knife and resumed chopping peppers. Shrugging, he said, "They both needed a blue crayon, so …"

"So, that was not the best way to solve that problem, Roland."

Beanie held in the sigh he wanted to exhale. It would be full of frustration and sarcasm and would make Noelle even more livid than she was already. He needed to de-escalate his wife's anger. Not make it worse.

"What was the best way to solve it?"

Noelle picked up her knife and sliced off a thin section of mango. "They need to learn to share. They won't be able to snap everything in half when there's only one of a specific thing, and they both want to use it at the same time."

"Elle, they're four and two," Beanie reminded his wife. "Sharing is not on their radar."

"Which is why we need to model the behavior," snapped Noelle, making several hard chops with the knife, nearly mangling the mango chunks.

"Hey, don't take it out on the mango," said Beanie. "We need that for the rice."

Noelle exhaled and put the knife down. "I'm sorry, okay."

"Don't apologize to me," said Beanie, eager to interject a bit of levity, hoping to lift his wife's dour mood. "You need to make amends with the mango."

Smiling, Noelle rolled her eyes. "You're very silly; you know that?"

"I've been called worse."

Shaking her head, Noelle said, "I didn't mean to be a smother. I just …"

"Just what?"

Lowering her voice, Noelle glanced at him and said, "I'm not upset with the mango."

"But you're upset about something?"

"My father …"

Beanie's gut twisted a bit. After the morning he'd wasted chasing false leads, he wasn't in the mood for a conversation about his wife's murderous father. Still, he was always curious about their contentious father-daughter relationship. The mystery behind his wife's animosity toward the man intrigued him, even more so because she flat-out refused to discuss the reason for her hatred.

"He wrote me a letter," said Noelle. "Gave it to mom when she went to visit him, and she forced me to take it."

Beanie asked, "What did it say?"

"I don't know." Noelle stared down toward the chunks of mango piled on the cutting board. "Didn't open it."

"Are you going to?"

"I don't need to open it to know what it says," said Noelle, looking at him. "He's a changed man. He goes to Bible study. He has seen the error of his ways. He wants to mend our relationship."

"But you don't want to," said Beanie.

"I can't …"

"Or you won't?"

Noelle looked away. "I don't want to get into it."

"Maybe you should get into it," suggested Beanie as he stared at his wife. "What's the issue with you and your father?"

"Are you really asking me that?" Noelle pinched the bridge of her nose. "You know what the issue is."

"Actually, no, I don't know," said Beanie. "You never want to talk about it."

"You're right. I don't," said Noelle. "So let's change the subject. How was your trip to Saint Xavier? Were you able to find out which one of those three guys killed Gavin de Grac?"

Beanie cut slowly into another pepper. He didn't want to change the subject. And yet he didn't want to press the issue. As much as he wanted to know why Noelle hated her father, he also didn't want to open up any old wounds that might cause his wife trauma or distress.

"It was a complete waste of time." Beanie sighed as he sidestepped to an overhead cabinet and opened the door. "None of the men had heard of Gavin de Grac or Zach Preston.

"That's so weird."

"Actually, it's not," said Beanie, removing a small bowl from the cabinet. "Well, Zach Preston is weird. I thought so the moment I met him. But that's what makes what he did not so weird."

Noelle frowned. "What do you mean?"

Beanie closed the cabinet and brought the bowl to the cutting board. "While I was talking to Preston, I pegged him as a gaslighting wacko. An attention seeker. One of those people who pretends to have information about a crime so they can feel important."

"Can't believe people do that and get away with it."

"They usually don't get charged with obstructing justice, though some of them should," said Beanie. "Guys like Preston know that the cops and reporters like me will check out the lead. And Preston knew he was giving me bogus information. Sending me on a wild goose chase for whatever reason."

"Sorry about that, babe," said Noelle, standing on her toes to give him a quick peck.

Beanie said, "Well, good things is, I have a lead that might pan out ... "

"What is it?" asked Noelle.

"Gavin's—"

"Daddy!" shouted Ethan. "Daddy! Evan won't give me the red crayon!"

Beanie glanced at his wife. "I promise I won't break the crayon."

"You know, it's probably not a bad idea."

Shocked, Beanie stared at his wife. "Wait. What?"

Laughing, Noelle said, "But let me do the honors this time ..."

17

A chill of anxious dread passed through Beanie as he stared at the man across the table in the booth where he sat.

Lime Shoes, whose real name Beanie didn't know and was too afraid to ask, was an old PC-5 gangster and confidential source. Each time Beanie visited the sinister, shrewd sixty-something, he was reminded of the first time he'd met the man.

The story still had the ability to rattle Beanie's nerves when he recalled it. After writing a story about the PC-5, which suggested that several low-level cartel members were robbing the elderly and infirm, Beanie had been kidnapped by a quartet of large, muscular henchmen, blindfolded, and driven to an unknown location.

When the blindfold was torn from his eyes, Beanie found himself face to face with an older man whose dark skin was lined with age and criminal accomplishments. Beanie was terrified by his scowl and shrewd gaze. While he tried not to soil himself and prayed he wouldn't be shot to death, the old man introduced himself.

His name, he told Beanie, was Lime Shoes. The PC-5 had dispatched him to explain that Beanie was not to write anything about the cartel that wasn't true. Lime Shoes' assignment was to make sure Beanie's stories accurately reflected the PC-5's involvement in whatever crime they were accused of committing. As a result, Lime Shoes had become Beanie's de facto confidential informant.

At one o'clock in the afternoon, outside the St. Killian sun blazed bright, but inside the Purple Gecko, where Beanie found himself two days later, the atmosphere was dim and gloomy. The scuzzy, sleazy dive bar, located in Handweg, was the unofficial base of Lime Shoes.

After dealing with several pressing stories and breaking news, Beanie could finally follow up on the lead given to him by Nora de Grac, who'd been threatened about the money her late husband owed to a bookie named Blitz.

Having no idea who Blitz was, Beanie figured the best person to ask was Lime Shoes. The gangster would know if Blitz was affiliated with the PC-5 or an independent contractor working with the cartel's permission.

"Been meaning to ask you," began Lime Shoes, his eyes narrowed.

Beanie braced himself, trying not to stare at the gangster's necklace. It was made from the teeth of a shark Lime Shoes was rumored to have killed after the beast attacked him.

"How's your little boy?" asked Lime Shoes, his grimace softening into a slight grin. "The oldest one? Ethan? That's his name, right?"

Slightly less nervous but still somewhat surprised, Beanie nodded. "Yeah, Ethan. He's four. And he's doing what he always does. Trying to get into as much mischief as possible."

Lime Shoes said, "I asked because I found out your Ethan goes to school with my grandbaby. Her name is Ambrosia."

Beanie's shock increased. Lime Shoes had a granddaughter? That meant the old gangster had at least one child. Maybe more. Beanie didn't know about Ambrosia, but then he wasn't aware of the names of Ethan's school friends. Noelle was involved in the boys' school activities and probably knew the little girl.

"I think Ethan is sweet on Amby. That's what they call her," said Lime Shoes, chuckling. "Ethan tried to cut one of her ponytails."

Mortified, Beanie shook his head. "He what? I'm sorry."

Lime Shoes laughed. "Well, she might have invited the attention. I think she tripped him during recess."

"She did?"

"The teacher says they're always picking at each other and fussing," said Lime Shoes. "Amby might be sweet on Ethan, too."

Beanie rubbed his jaw. He wasn't sure how to feel about his son being sweet on Lime Shoes' granddaughter. On the one hand, he thought it was harmless. Ethan and Amby were kids. Only four years old. But on the other hand, the fact that they were four years old and might be sweet on each other jarred him. Because they were kids. What did four-year-old kids know about liking each other in a romantic way?

"Anyway," said Lime Shoes. "I'm sure you're not here to talk about your son and my granddaughter, so ..."

"Just have a question or two," said Beanie.

"Or three or four," said Lime Shoes.

Beanie forced a laugh to combat the slight, sly panic that snaked through him. Whenever he had to talk to the old gangster, he experienced a fissure of trepidation. After all, the man had been in the cartel for most of his life. He was a confidential source, but he was also a criminal. Beanie remained aware of the bodyguards stationed throughout the bar, ready to spray bullets if necessary.

"Do you know anything about a bookie called Blitz?"

Lime Shoes picked up the tumbler filled with dark amber liquid and took a sip. "Why do you want to know about him? You playing the goats now or something?"

Beanie shook his head. "I'm working on a follow-up story about the guy found dead on Mango Beach. I got a lead about Blitz. He might have had something to do with the murder."

Frowning, Lime Shoes said, "I thought the cops had arrested the dude's neighbor."

"They did," said Beanie. "And he seems guilty, but ..."

"But let me guess," said Lime Shoes. "The victim had a gambling problem and owed Blitz money."

"One of Blitz's associates threatened the victim's wife," said Beanie. "The message was sent a few weeks before the victim was killed."

Lime Shoes took another sip of whiskey. "And you think Blitz shot the guy?"

Shrugging, Beanie said, "I'm not sure. But I figured I might check it out. The victim's wife wants me to look into whether the bookie might have killed her husband."

Exhaling, Lime Shoes said, "Afraid I can't tell you much about Blitz. Don't know the man personally, but he's got permission from the cartel to run his operation. For a fee, of course."

Beanie nodded. Most independent crooks with no ties to the PC-5 had to pay a "permission tax" to the cartel if they wanted to commit their crimes or risk the wrath of the gang.

"Blitz is small-time," said Lime Shoes. "Doesn't cause problems."

"Which means he probably didn't kill Gavin de Grac," said Beanie.

"Didn't say that," said Lime Shoes. "Said I don't really know the man. But I know someone who does …"

18

Beanie hated walking across the beach in his driving shoes.

With each step, he kicked up sugary sand around the hem of his ankles. Sand that would end up in the car, making it necessary for a stop at the car wash to use the vacuum. Normally, a trip to Rouge Beach would take place on the weekend. He, Noelle, and the boys would put on their bathing suits and pack large bags with plenty of towels, sunscreen, and snacks.

Once they arrived, Beanie would lug their beach chairs and an old umbrella from the car. Noelle would carry the bags, and the boys would sprint toward the Caribbean Sea, excited and entranced by the shimmering turquoise waters. They would ignore warnings to slow down, be careful, and wait so that Daddy could go into the water with them. These nice family outings would take place under blue skies dotted with white, cottony clouds and bright sunshine.

But today was not a postcard-perfect Palmchat Island day. Humid and overcast, the atmosphere was heavy with sudden gusty breezes and the damp, sharp smell of approaching storms.

And his wife and kids weren't around. And it was Tuesday. His trip to the beach had nothing to do with family bonding. He was looking for a man named Knight. According to Lime Shoes, Knight—the old gangster only knew the man by the name Knight and didn't know if Knight was a first or a last or a middle name—was one of Blitz the bookie's collectors. From Beanie's limited knowledge, a collector was a small-time hood who paid a visit to people with outstanding debts they owed to the bookie. If the person didn't have the money, the collector might threaten them or rough them up. Try to scare the cash out of them, so to speak.

Lime Shoes had told Beanie he could find Knight's kiosk set up between a fruit stand and a guy who sold timeshares. Beanie spotted the fruit stand first. Behind the splintered wooden counter, an older man and a young guy took orders for smoothies. A blender whirred as Beanie excused himself through the line of tourists.

Right of the fruit stand were three rickety kiosks loaded with hundreds of T-shirts in all colors and sizes. A trio of Europeans, wrapped in yellow and white beach towels, haggled with a fair-skinned Palmchatter. Beanie waited a few feet away, watching the guy—Knight, he assumed—trying to convince the tourists to make a purchase. Knight's presentation, which was overdramatic and punctuated by overexcited gestures, seemed to entertain the three women, but eventually, they shook their heads and laughed as they drifted away.

"You win some, you lose some, right?" Beanie angled toward the kiosk owner.

The man, who had scowled as he watched the women leave, immediately turned his frown upside down and focused on Beanie.

"But their loss is your gain, brother," said the man, beckoning Beanie closer to the kiosks. "Today, and today only, I am offering a great deal. Buy three, get one free. Only $15. Best bargain on the beach. You can't beat this deal with a stick. A street vendor or some old auntie with a stall at the flea market will charge you five dollars a T-shirt. That's four shirts for $20."

Beanie nodded.

"With me, you get four shirts for fifteen dollars."

Beanie was fairly certain Knight knew he wasn't a tourist, but he figured the man was always on his grind and saw everyone, even locals, as potential customers

"Actually," Beanie cut in, interrupting the spiel. "I just have a few questions for you."

Smiling and nodding, the man said, "I figured you would."

"You did?"

"I know what you're going to ask."

"You do?" asked Beanie, but he doubted it.

"Okay, first off, this is quality cotton," said the man, his pale gray eyes earnest. "This is not that cheap, fake cotton they sell down at the flea market. You can wash these shirts. I guarantee you they will not shrink."

Again, Beanie doubted the man. "Is it pre-shrunk cotton?"

Knight shook his head. "This is quality cotton, man. And all my shirts are made in the Palmchat Islands, so you'll be supporting our local economy, brother."

Beanie was sure he'd seen the same shirts at Palm-Mart, and suspected Knight did not have a legitimate supplier, but he wasn't there to question the man about possibly stolen T-shirts.

"Actually, I have a question about Blitz," said Beanie.

The man paused and blinked several times. "Who is … what was the name? Blink? Blick?"

"Blitz," corrected Beanie.

The man looked away. "Who is that?"

"I think you know," said Beanie. "You're Knight, right?"

The man gave Beanie a sharp, suspicious look. "Who's asking?"

Beanie introduced himself, then said, "I'm working on a story about a man found dead on Mango Beach."

"What's that got to do with me?"

"The victim was Gavin de Grac," said Beanie, staring at Knight, scanning his expression for furtive dishonesty.

"That name supposed to mean something to me?"

"Mr. de Grac's widow, Nora de Grac, got some threatening messages about outstanding gambling debts that Gavin owed," said Beanie. "You know anything about that?"

"I know I didn't call and threaten nobody," said Knight. "And if someone said I did, they're lying."

"But you work for Blitz, right?"

"Who told you that?" demanded Knight, a challenge in his gaze.

Weary of the back-and-forth cat-and-mouse, Beanie said, "Listen, I'm not interested in a quote or a comment from you. I'm trying to figure out if Blitz had something to do with Gavin de Grac's death. Maybe Blitz killed Gavin because Gavin didn't pay his gambling debts. Does that seem possible?"

Knight turned to a kiosk and reached into an open box filled with T-shirts. He pulled one of the T-shirts out and folded it. "I don't know nothing about nobody found dead on a beach or whether Blitz is the reason why that man is dead. But I can tell you what I have heard about Blitz, allegedly ..."

"And what's that?"

Knight pulled another T-shirt from the box, folded it, and found a place for it on a shelf already overstuffed with shirts. "Blitz doesn't play when it comes to his money. If you owe him, you better pay up. Because he will come after you ..."

19

"I know Ambrosia," said Noelle, smiling. "Ethan's little girlfriend."

Beanie frowned as he rinsed the dinner plate he'd just washed. "His little girlfriend?"

"I think he likes her," said Noelle, dunking a drinking glass into the sudsy dishwater. "He's always teasing her. She's really pretty. I think she likes him, too, because she teases him right back."

"Wait. What do you mean they like each other? Like each other in what way?"

Noelle shrugged. "You know, like a little crush."

"A crush?" Beanie gaped at his wife. "They are four years old. What do they know about having a crush? They shouldn't be having those kinds of feelings. Ethan should think girls are gross and yucky and dumb."

Rolling her eyes, Noelle passed him the glass she'd just washed. "Roland, don't be such a dad, okay?"

"Don't be a dad?" As he rinsed the glass, Beanie found it ironic that his wife, a notorious self-admitted "smother," would accuse him of overreacting.

"Relax, okay? It's harmless. Nothing serious." Noelle dunked two plates into the dishwater. "And you're right. They don't know what those feelings are. They won't know until they're much older. Then we can worry."

Beanie sighed. "Maybe by then, Ethan will be interested in someone else instead of Ambrosia."

"Why do you say that?"

Taking the plates his wife had just cleaned, Beanie said, "Because I don't want to get on her grandfather's bad side if Ethan breaks her heart. I mean, you know who her grandfather is, right?"

Noelle nodded. "Lime Shoes. Ambrosia's mom, Amber, and I have talked about the things we have in common besides preschoolers in the same class."

"Things in common meaning …"

"Gangster fathers … "

Beanie rinsed the plates. "You know, I was shocked when Lime Shoes mentioned Ambrosia. He'd never opened up about his family before. Didn't know he had a family."

"He probably never mentioned Ambrosia because he didn't know she existed until a year ago."

"What do you mean?"

Noelle explained that Amber had only recently decided to introduce Lime Shoes to his granddaughter. She and Noelle had discussed allowing their fathers to know their grandchildren. Amber decided Ambrosia should get to know Lime Shoes because her grandmother, Amber's mom, had passed away.

"Because of Amber's mom's death, she felt it was time for Ambrosia and Lime Shoes to meet," said Noelle.

"But you still don't think the boys should know their grandfather."

Noelle gave him a sharp look. "Amber's father is not an assassin."

"And Lime Shoes is not a Boy Scout."

"Compared to my father, he is," retorted Noelle. "The difference between me and Amber is that Lime Shoes shielded her from the PC-5. He had a clear separation between work and home life. Amber didn't even know her dad was in the cartel until about three or four years ago."

Beanie was shocked. "Really?"

"When Amber was a little girl, Lime Shoes sent Amber and her mother to live with his sisters in Barbados," said Noelle, abandoning the dishes as she turned from the sink. "He would visit them there. And then, Amber went to university in London. Lime Shoes never exposed Amber to cartel life, unlike Josue Chartres, who bragged and boasted about being the top Death List assassin."

The solemn scowl on his wife's pretty face angered and worried Beanie. He felt horrible for Noelle. He couldn't imagine what it was like, growing up with a notorious father who killed people. He hated that Noelle's memories of her father always caused her mental trauma and anguish.

"Babe, can you finish the dishes?" asked Noelle. "I have a bit of a headache."

"Of course," said Beanie, giving her a quick kiss before she left the kitchen.

Staring into the dishwater, Beanie reflected on his wife's tone and posture as she'd spoken about her similarities with Amber. He'd heard hints of envy and resentment. Noelle's primary anger was directed at her father, but Beanie wondered if she was jealous of the way Lime Shoes had protected his daughter. Maybe Noelle wished that her father had shielded her from the gang's violent influence.

Absently, Beanie finished the remaining dishes, washing, drying, and then replacing them in the overhead kitchen cabinets.

20

"Why hasn't Janvier arrested Stanley Iris?" Beanie asked Officer Fields after the men had spent a few moments chatting amicably about Fields's dismal love life and their favorite cricket team's dismal record.

"Believe it or not, Detective Janvier is not quite sure that Stanley Iris is the killer."

Beanie didn't believe it. "Are you serious? The evidence is pretty compelling."

"Well, it's the evidence that's giving Janvier pause," said Fields.

Beanie's disbelief turned to outright shock. "You mean to tell me that Janvier is actually considering the evidence and not blindly following his own unconscious bias?"

"Appears so."

"I thought the evidence against Stanley Iris was solid."

"So did I," said Fields. "But Janvier asked the crime scene lab for more tests. On what? I don't know. He tries not to share things with me because he doesn't want me talking to you, but I have friends in the lab. So when I find out, I'll let you know."

"I appreciate that," said Beanie. "Hey, before you go. Not that I want to admit it, but Janvier might be right about Stanley Iris. I found out that Gavin de Grac owed money to a bookie called Blitz. And, allegedly, according to my source, Blitz has been known to hurt people who don't pay him."

"I know Blitz," said Fields. "And he does more than just hurt people who don't pay him. We questioned him last year about the murder of one of his clients. Blitz's ex-wife gave him an alibi, but we had a feeling she was afraid not to if you know what I mean."

"Yeah, I do," said Beanie.

Fields said, "I'll see what I can find out. If Blitz is involved, then he probably did it."

After the phone call with Fields, Beanie leaned back and glanced toward the ceiling. With Fields checking out the bookie Blitz, Beanie let his mind wander to the evidence that had given Janvier pause.

Considering the evidence against Stanley Iris – the murder weapon belonged to Iris. The man had sent the victim threatening messages. He didn't have an alibi for the night de Grac was killed — Beanie would have thought Janvier would consider the case closed. Which evidence had caused the detective to hold off on arresting Stanley Iris? Or was it possible that new evidence had been discovered? Maybe Janvier had spoken to a new witness? Or maybe—

The desk phone rang.

"Roland Bean," said Beanie, pressing the receiver against his ear.

"I think you should know that Stanley Iris did not kill Gavin de Grac," announced the caller, a woman with a high-pitched, shrill tone.

A fissure of disbelief passed through Beanie. Part of him wanted to sarcastically reply that he agreed with the caller, and the lead detective on the case felt the same way. Another part of him wondered why so many people were so sure that Iris wasn't the killer. Was Stanley Iris asking people to advocate on his behalf? Then again, Beanie had doubts about Iris' guilt, also.

Grabbing his mouse, Beanie faced his computer and opened a Word document to take notes.

Pressing the speaker button, he placed the receiver on the base and asked, "And who's calling, please?"

After a moment's hesitation, the woman said, "A concerned citizen who does not want to see an innocent man go to jail."

Of course, thought Beanie, but he asked, "And how do you know that Stanley Iris didn't kill Gavin de Grac?"

"Because Gavin de Grac was killed by a hitman."

Beanie stopped typing. "A hitman?"

"A man was paid to kill Gavin de Grac," said the concerned citizen who didn't want to see an innocent man go to jail.

"What's the hitman's name?" Beanie leaned back in his squeaky leather chair and stared at the desk phone.

"Tommy Mizell," said the caller. "He's a janitor at the building where I work."

"What building is that?" asked Beanie, reaching for a pen and his sticky notes.

"The Orange Building," said the woman.

Beanie shuddered. He knew that building. The color of a Dreamsicle, the three-story structure housed several office suites, one of which had belonged to a company called SORE, Inc. The business advertised itself as a clinic to help those struggling with addictions. The truth about the clinic, however, was scandalous and sinister.

"I work for an insurance company," said the caller. "One of our customers took out a $100,000 double indemnity life insurance policy on Gavin de Grac two months ago. This customer also asked Tommy Mizell to kill Gavin de Grac."

"And did Tommy Mizell kill de Grac?"

"He must have," said the caller. "Gavin de Grac is dead."

Suspicious of the woman's story, Beanie asked, "Have you told the police this?"

"Yes, I did," said the caller. "But they haven't called me back. I don't know if they're investigating what I told them or not. I've called the station several times, but I keep getting the runaround. So, I figured I'd get the press involved. Maybe if you write the story, the police will be shamed into doing their jobs. They're supposed to get criminals off the street. Not let people get away with murder. Tommy Mizell needs to be in jail. And so does Nora de Grac."

Beanie sat forward. "Wait a minute. What was that about Nora de Grac?"

"Nora de Grac should go to jail," said the caller. "She hired Tommy Mizell to kill her husband."

21

"The secretary's name is Trina Walters," Officer Fields said, then took a sip of his latte.

After a sip of his cappuccino, Beanie placed the large cup on the wooden bistro table he and Fields had been lucky to snag, considering the massive crowd milling about Pourciau Square at three in the afternoon. The day was gorgeous. A perfect picture of paradise. Beanie figured people wanted to enjoy the lush tropical beauty after several days of overcast skies and on-and-off rain.

Earlier that morning, Beanie had called Fields to discuss the phone call he'd received the previous day, during which an anonymous concerned citizen had accused Nora de Grac of hiring a janitor named Tommy Mizell to kill Gavin de Grac.

Beanie remained skeptical of the claim, but after a bit of speculation with his coworkers, Stevie and Caleb, he'd decided to confer with Fields about it. Turned out, Fields had information for him. Beanie suggested a Hullabaloo Coffee break at the coffee shop's pop-up kiosk in Pourciau Square.

"Ms. Walters has called the station several times," said Fields, shaking his head.

"So, is Ms. Walters' claim the reason why Janvier hasn't arrested Stanley Iris?" asked Beanie. "Is Janvier looking into Nora de Grac and Tommy Mizell?"

"Not that I know of," said Fields. "Janvier remains less than forthcoming about this investigation. I'm not sure if he sent someone out to talk to Mizell."

"You think he should?" asked Beanie. "I was wondering if Trina Walters is just trying to get Nora de Grac in trouble."

Fields took another sip of coffee. "Why do you think that? What did she tell you? I haven't taken any of her calls."

Recalling the conversation with the woman who'd referred to herself as a concerned citizen, Beanie said, "Trina claimed that Gavin and Nora's marriage was on the rocks. She said they couldn't stand each other."

"How did she know?" asked Fields.

Beanie sighed, remembering Trina's—the concerned citizen's—answer to that very question.

"I know because Gavin told me," said the concerned citizen. "Me and him were together."

Beanie had been flabbergasted. "Together?"

"Me and Gavin was in love," she'd said. "He was going to divorce Nora, and me and him was going to get married. Nora was furious, so she paid Tommy Mizell to kill Gavin."

"And how do you know that Nora paid Tommy to kill Gavin?"

"Because Tommy told me," she'd said. "Me and Tommy are friends. We talk all the time. And Tommy and Nora were fooling around. That's why she asked him to kill Gavin."

With a long exhale and a chuckle, Officer Fields shook his head. "Sometimes, I'm glad I'm not married. Sounds like a mess."

"What about a motive for murder?" asked Beanie, finishing his coffee. "Sound like that?"

Fields shrugged. "If it's true, I suppose it does give Nora a motive. And after what I found out from the crime lab, Janvier might want to take a look at the widow."

His interest piqued, Beanie asked, "Are you talking about Janvier's evidence tests?"

Fields nodded. "Initially, you know, we recovered Stanley Iris' gun from the crime scene, along with shell casings which indicated that the gun had been fired."

"Into de Grac's gut," interjected Beanie.

"Actually, that's not true," said Fields.

Beanie was confused. "What?"

"Gavin de Grac was not killed with Stanley Iris' gun, it turns out," said Fields.

"I don't understand."

Fields explained, "The evidence that gave Janvier pause was this—the bullets removed from Gavin de Grac did not come from Stanley Iris' gun."

"Are you serious?"

"Gavin de Grac was not shot with Stanley Iris' gun," reiterated Fields. "He was shot with a different gun, according to the ballistics report. So far, Janvier hasn't been able to trace the gun, based on the bullets, or recover the murder weapon."

"So Stanley Iris' gun is not the murder weapon?"

Fields shook his head. "No. But Stanley Iris' gun was discharged. Shell casings and bullets were recovered along with the gun, which I just found out. Told you Janvier was being very secretive. Here's another detail he kept close to the vest: Gavin de Grac had gunpower residue on his hands. And, de Grac's prints were on Stanley Iris' gun."

Beanie rubbed his jaw. "Wait. That sounds like a gunfight."

Fields nodded slowly. "Doesn't it? The way Janvier figures it, and I agree, Gavin de Grac and his killer got into some kind of argument or skirmish or whatever. Gavin de Grac fired his weapon—"

"Which was Stanley Iris' gun," said Beanie.

"And who knows if de Grac was the aggressor or fired back in self-defense," said Fields. "What we do know is that his killer was a much better shot than he was …"

22

Sitting across from Beanie at a table in the *Palmchat Gazette* breakroom, Caleb Olivier said, "I have to say that Detective Janvier seems to be on top of his investigation into Gavin de Grac's murder."

A few days had passed since Fields dropped the bombshell about Gavin de Grac. During that time, Beanie had written two follow-up stories, one of which was a popular interactive article where he took a video of the actual crime scene on Mango Beach.

Sitting to Beanie's right, Stevie Bishop agreed. "Normally, he would have completely ignored the fact that the bullets recovered from de Grac's body didn't match the gun found at the crime scene."

Beanie nodded. "Janvier would have found some way to convince himself that Stanley Iris' gun was the murder weapon. He would have arrested another innocent person. And then when he got to the point where he couldn't ignore the evidence, he would have shrugged and offered no apology for his short-sightedness and confirmation bias."

Stevie chuckled. "Maybe your critique of his investigative skills got to him."

Caleb said, "Might have inspired the man to do better."

Beanie shook his head and took a sip of his third cup of coffee of the day. "I doubt that. Anyway … now that it appears Stanley Iris is not the murderer—"

"And I guess he told you the truth about Gavin de Grac taking his gun," said Stevie.

"I think he did," said Beanie.

"I was wrong about that," admitted Caleb. "When Iris told you that de Grac had stolen his gun, I thought that was ridiculous."

Beanie said, "Well, it's looking like Stanley Iris didn't kill Gavin. So who did?"

"My money is on the bookie," said Caleb. "I've heard about that guy. Cops think he killed a client."

"Fields told me," said Beanie. "He was questioned but never charged with anything because his ex-wife gave him an alibi."

Caleb snorted. "Yeah, well, like I said … that bookie is bad news. And Gavin probably knew that, which is why he took Stanley Iris' gun. He needed protection. Gavin had to have known Blitz was out to get him over that gambling debt. And the fact that the cops haven't been able to trace the gun makes me think it's a PC-5 ghost gun. Blitz would know how to get a weapon like that."

Stevie said, "I think it was Nora de Grac."

"You believe Trina Walters?" asked Beanie. "The secretary turned concerned citizen."

Nodding, Stevie said, "Romantic rivalry is a powerful motive for murder. You know, Nora is upset because Gavin is interested in another woman and wants to divorce her. So she wants revenge. She wants him dead because he wounded her pride and made her feel like she was less of a woman."

"And she figured, why not profit off his death," said Beanie. "I actually think that's plausible. I did a public record search and found out that Nora de Grac filed for divorce several times, but she appears to have called it off both times. In her divorce petition, she claimed Gavin was abusive, which corroborates Trina's claim that the marriage was basically over."

Caleb shook his head. "But what proof do you have that this secretary is telling the truth? How do you know that she and Gavin were fooling around? How do you know that the secretary didn't kill Gavin?"

Frowning, Stevie asked, "Why would Trina Walters kill Gavin de Grac if she was in love with him?"

"Because what if Gavin wasn't in love with her?" suggested Caleb. "Maybe Gavin was just fooling around on his wife with no intentions to leave Nora, especially if Nora called off the divorce twice. Sounds like a man who made mistakes but asked for forgiveness."

Warming to Caleb's theory, Beanie said, "You think Trina might have killed Gavin because he wouldn't leave his wife?"

Shrugging, Stevie said, "A case of … if I can't have him, then you can't either."

Beanie sighed. "But what about the life insurance policy Nora took out on Gavin?"

"According to Trina," said Caleb. "But is that true? Have you been able to confirm that Nora took out the policy?"

Shaking his head, Beanie said, "I haven't spoken to Nora about Trina's claims."

"Maybe you should," said Caleb. "And, if possible, you should have a conversation with Tommy Mizell. You have to find out if the man really did accept money to kill Gavin de Grac."

"He won't tell Beanie if he did," said Stevie.

"Of course, he won't," said Caleb, scowling at Stevie. "And Beanie won't just come out and ask the man. He'll be subtle and sly with his questions."

"I will?" Beanie chuckled, not sure he could pull off the calculated, cunning questioning Caleb suggested.

Caleb said, "You will if you hope to get honest answers."

Twenty minutes later, back at his desk, Beanie saw he'd missed a phone call, but the person had left a message.

Dropping down into the squeaky leather chair, Beanie pressed the button to retrieve the voice message.

"Hey, it's Fields ... just wanted to let you know I checked out that bookie, Blitz. By the way, his real name is Victor Trimarco. Looks like he didn't have anything to do with Gavin de Grac's murder. Trimarco was in jail in the Bahamas on the Fourth of July. He's been locked up since March ..."

23

"I can't believe she thought I was actually gonna kill a man for a lousy two thousand dollars," said Tommy Mizell as he swiped a mop from left to right across the speckled tile in the narrow hallway.

Beanie had found the janitor on the third floor of the Orange Building. After a quick lunch at the Loco Goat food truck, parked in a row of other trucks on the street behind the Pourciau Bank, Beanie walked to the building where he encountered an old high school friend working security behind the front desk.

Beanie chatted with the security guard, making plans to meet at a bar to watch a cricket match, and then stated his business. He was there to talk to the janitor, Tommy Mizell. The security guard had told him where he might find Mizell.

Yesterday, after discussing Trina Walters' claim with Caleb and Stevie and then finding out that the bookie Blitz could no longer be considered a suspect, Beanie started to wonder if de Grac's death had been solicited.

Despite Caleb's suggestion that Beanie use sly subtleness when questioning Mizell, Beanie opted for a more direct approach. Sometimes, when a question came out of nowhere, a person's initial reaction could speak volumes. Beanie started by asking Mizell if it was true that he and Nora de Grac were having an affair and Nora had hired him to kill her husband, Gavin. He figured Mizell would stammer a denial or remain suspiciously silent. Either of those responses might mean that Trina Walters had been telling the truth. On the other hand, if Mizell appeared genuinely shocked and offended, Beanie might be able to conclude that Trina Walters had lied.

As it turned out, Beanie had been shocked and stunned speechless for a moment when Mizell laughed and then said, "Me and Nora wasn't fooling around. She's old enough to be my momma. However, I was hired to kill Gavin de Grac. But not by his wife."

"I don't understand," Beanie had said. "So … wait, Nora de Grac didn't hire you?"

Shaking his head, Mizell said, "Trina Walters hired me."

Beanie had been floored, and still was, listening to the janitor recount the sordid story.

"Man, it cost more than that for me to risk my immortal soul," said Mizell, cackling under his breath.

"So, you turned Trina Walters down?" asked Beanie.

"No, I actually took Trina's money," said Mizell, dragging the mop along the floorboard. "That two thousand came in handy. The electric company was threatening to cut my lights off. They'd sent me a notice because I was two months past due, so I was able to get caught up. And still had some money left over. Took my girl to the Aerie Islands for the weekend."

Beanie asked, "So Trina thinks you killed Gavin?"

Mizell shook his head. "She knows I didn't. She asked me to get rid of de Grac last month."

"But obviously, you didn't."

"Nope." Mizell laughed as he continued mopping. "Trina was mad as a wild mountain goat. But what could she do? Go to the cops? And tell them what? A man stole two thousand dollars from me that I paid him to kill my secret lover?"

Beanie asked, "Do you know why Trina Walters wanted Gavin dead? She told me that de Grac was going to leave his wife and marry her."

Mizell stopped mopping and laughed out loud. "Man, I knew that girl was crazy. Mr. de Grac was not going to leave his wife. That's why Trina wanted him dead. She said he lied to her. Made her think he loved her and wanted to be with her. But he didn't. That old dude was just taking advantage of Trina's daddy issues. When she caught a clue and realized he wasn't going to leave his wife, she wanted me to kill him."

Confused, Beanie asked. "So, why would Trina tell the cops that Nora hired you to kill de Grac? Wasn't she afraid that you would snitch on her to the cops?"

Nodding, Mizell propped an elbow on top of the mop. "As I said, Trina was upset that I scammed her. But after Gavin's neighbor killed him, she came up with another scheme. She wanted me to tell the cops that Nora de Grac paid me to kill Gavin."

"But you refused?" asked Beanie.

"Man, I wasn't going to tell the cops that I got hired to kill somebody," said Tommy Mizell, resuming his mopping. "Like I told Trina, it don't matter that I didn't kill the man. I took the money. That's still a crime. So then Trina tries to blackmail me. She tells me that if I don't do what she wants, then she'll tell the cops that Mrs. de Grac hired me to kill Gavin."

"Which she did," said Beanie.

"The cops questioned me," said Mizell. "I told them I had no idea what Trina was talking about."

"You didn't point the finger back at Trina?"

"Man, I don't snitch," said Mizell. "Besides, it would have been my word against hers. But I could have told the cops what Trina told me after she realized I took her money but didn't kill her boyfriend."

"What did Trina tell you?" asked Beanie.

Mizell stopped mopping again and said, "Trina said she would kill Gavin herself …"

24

The next morning, sitting in his tiny cubicle at the *Palmchat Gazette* offices, Beanie took a sip of his first cup of coffee of the day.

A Word file with his notes on the Gavin de Grac murder case was opened on his computer screen.

Beanie stared at the sentence he'd bolded and highlighted: Who killed Gavin de Grac?

Beneath that sentence was the word, SUSPECTS, typed in all caps. Rubbing his jaw, Beanie propped an elbow on his small desk and considered the list of names.

Stanley Iris

Blitz, the bookie

Tommy Mizell

He supposed, at this point, each of the names could be removed from the list.

At one time, Stanley Iris had been the main suspect. The man certainly passed the motive, means, and opportunity test. Gavin de Grac's cranky neighbor was livid about a palm tree and had, in the past, been arrested for attacking other residents. He owned a gun and didn't have an alibi for the night de Grac had been killed.

But, despite his beef with de Grac, the evidence against Iris hadn't held up. The man's gun, as it turned out, was not the murder weapon. Of course, there was always the possibility that Iris had shot de Grac with a ghost gun after de Grac had stolen Iris' gun. However, that scenario was a bit too farfetched. As was the motive of killing a man over a dispute about a palm tree. The man didn't have an alibi, but Beanie had a feeling the old coot had been at home when de Grac was killed. Or possibly out in his yard, obsessing over the plants and bushes in his lawn.

Beanie felt confident he could strike Stanley Iris' name from the suspect list.

Blitz, the bookie, was another suspect that was no longer a suspect. Removing Blitz was easy. The man had been in jail when Gavin de Grac was killed. Blitz hadn't escaped jail, traveled to the Palmchat Islands to kill de Grac, and then returned to jail. The idea was ridiculous. However, it wasn't ridiculous to think that, from his jail cell, Blitz had ordered the murder of Gavin de Grac. Knight, the bookie's collector, could have secured a ghost gun and used it to kill de Grac.

Dropping his gaze to Tommy Mizell's name, Beanie considered the janitor.

Mizell had admitted that he'd been hired to kill Gavin de Grac. But he hadn't killed the man. Instead, he'd scammed Trina Walters. He'd taken her money, used it to pay his electricity bill, and took his girlfriend on a weekend getaway. Beanie considered that Mizell could have lied to him. For all Beanie knew, Mizell might have lied about stealing Trina's money. He could have fibbed about not having the guts to kill. He might have earned the two thousand dollars. His suggestion that Trina Walters had killed her secret lover could have been his attempt to deflect guilt from himself.

Sighing, Beanie leaned back in his chair.

He wasn't sure what to think about Mizell. The murder-for-hire situation between the janitor and the side chick was basically a "he said, she said" situation. Mizell claimed he took the money but didn't murder the victim. Beanie was certain that if he questioned Trina Walters, she would outright deny paying someone to kill her boyfriend. There would be no way to truly tell who was lying.

Beanie looked at his suspect list again.

With his mouse, he highlighted Stanley Iris and Blitz the bookie, then hit the delete button. He typed a new name in place of the suspects he'd removed.

Trina Walters

Mizell claimed Trina Walters had told him she would kill Gavin herself. Could that be true? Possibly. Trina had a motive. Mizell said she'd been hurt and vengeful when she realized Gavin wasn't going to leave Nora. According to the old saying, the scorned woman could be worse than hell. Trina could have shot Gavin because he'd lied to her. Played with her affections and emotions. It might have been a crime of passion. Again, the major questions were, could Trina have gotten a ghost gun? And did she have an alibi?

Beanie stroked his jaw. He would start with trying to determine if Trina Walters had an alibi and then—

The desk phone buzzed.

Glancing at the caller ID, Beanie read his boss's name—Vivian Thomas-Bronson.

"Hey, Viv," said Beanie, wondering why the Managing Editor was calling two hours before the daily ten a.m. staff meeting.

"Come to my office."

A hint of alarm washed over Beanie. His boss's curt, no-nonsense tone concerned him. He hoped there wasn't a problem with one of his stories. As he walked to Vivian's office, Beanie wondered if he'd gotten some facts wrong. Or maybe he'd misquoted an important witness. Last thing he wanted was to expose the paper to a libel lawsuit.

Seconds later, Beanie knocked on Vivian's half-opened door.

"Come on in ..."

Beanie entered. "What's up?"

Facing her computer, fingers flying over her keyboard, Vivian said, "My source at the St. Killian Police Department just emailed me. Janvier made an arrest in the murder of Gavin de Grac."

Relief replaced Beanie's unfounded dread. He asked, "Who's the suspect?"

Glancing at him, Vivian said, "A man named ... Zachary Preston."

25

"So the guy who sent you on the wild goose chase is actually the killer?" asked Noelle as she took a seat on the settee at the foot of the bed.

"Apparently," said Beanie, leaning back on the pillows stacked against the headboard as he scrolled through his social media feeds on his cell phone.

"That is so crazy."

"I think it makes perfect sense," said Beanie, stopping at a photo of an old college buddy. "As soon as I met Zach Preston, I didn't trust him. Something was off about the guy. His story seemed like complete fiction."

"He told you that one of the three St. X guys killed Gavin de Grac, right?"

Beanie admired the college buddy's photo, which showed him standing on the bow of a boat, beaming broadly as he held up a marlin he'd caught. "Three guys who'd never heard of Gavin de Grac or Zach Preston."

"I wonder why he chose those three guys," said Noelle.

Beanie glanced at his wife as she massaged cocoa-scented shea butter onto her arms and shoulders. "I have no idea. He might have picked their names out of the phone book."

"That's awful," said Noelle. "He could have caused serious problems for them. Imagine if he'd gone to the cops? The police might have investigated them. They might have been forced to provide alibis."

"Yeah, well, those guys don't have to worry about the cops," said Beanie, scrolling again. "Zachary Preston is behind bars."

"Are you going to interview him?"

"Vivian wanted me to," said Beanie, pausing at a picture of his cousin, Larry, who had an arm draped around his American girlfriend. "But Zach Preston refused to speak with the media, which is his right. And honestly, I don't even want to talk to the guy. Not interested in more of his lies."

"What's the evidence against Zach Preston?" asked Noelle.

"Vivian's source didn't give her that information," said Beanie. "But I'm meeting with Fields tomorrow morning. Hopefully, he'll have the details for me."

Noelle screwed the cap back on the shea butter. "Speaking of Fields …"

"What about him?"

"He's still single, right?"

Thrown by the question, Beanie stared at his wife. "Why are you asking me that?"

"Does he have a girlfriend, or not?" asked Noelle, staring back at him.

"I don't think so," said Beanie. "I mean, I think he's single. Why do you want to know about Fields' love life?"

Giving him a mischievous smile, Noelle climbed over the footboard and crawled toward him. "Well, I was talking to Amber …"

"Amber?"

"Ambrosia's mom," said Noelle, stretching out next to Beanie.

"Lime Shoes' daughter?" asked Beanie.

"I think we should fix her up with Damon Fields," said Noelle.

"Huh?" Beanie sat up and looked down at his wife. "Why?"

"Because she's ready to start dating again," said Noelle. "Things didn't work out with her and Ambrosia's dad. And she's looking for a nice guy. Someone handsome but caring and compassionate. And funny."

"You think Fields is handsome?"

Noelle sighed and propped herself up on her elbow. "We could double date. Dinner at Dizzy Jenny's. You invite Fields. I'll invite Amber."

Beanie shook his head. "Not a good idea."

"Why not?" demanded Noelle. "Didn't you tell me that Fields wants to get married?"

"I told you that Fields' mom and his sisters are always pressuring him about getting married," said Beanie.

"Same thing," said Noelle, turning over onto her back. "Anyway, Amber is really pretty. And she's nice. Smart. Personable. A great mom. I think Fields would like her."

"I don't think Fields would like me getting involved in his love life," said Beanie.

Exhaling, Noelle said, "Will you just ask him?"

"Fields is more than capable of finding a woman to go out with," said Beanie. "I don't want to play matchmaker. He might get offended. And I need to keep him as a source. You know Janvier won't tell me anything. And if Fields stops talking to me because I butted into his personal life, Vivian will fire me."

"Roland ..." Noelle shook her head. "Will you stop being melodramatic? Just tell Fields that your wife has someone she thinks he might be interested in getting to know and find out if he's interested. If he is, great."

"Okay, fine," said Beanie, laying back on the pillows. "I will ask Fields if he's interested in being set up, but if he's not, then ..."

Noelle said, "Then it'll be his loss ..."

26

After his early morning breakfast meeting with Officer Damon Fields, Beanie returned to the *Palmchat Gazette* offices, eager to write a follow-up story with the details Fields had shared regarding the arrest of Zach Preston.

Striding through the newspaper's foyer, Beanie smiled at the receptionist. "Good morning, Millie."

"Morning, Beanie," said Millie, returning the smile. "Oh, you have a visitor."

Beanie stepped to the parabola-shaped receptionist desk. "A visitor?"

"In the conference room."

Confused, Beanie asked, "Who is it?"

Millie said, "Zachary Preston."

Several moments later, Beanie walked into the conference room. A powerful feeling of déjà-vu gripped him. Weeks ago, when he'd encountered the man sitting at the far end of the large oblong table, Beanie had been intrigued and suspicious. Today, he was just suspicious. As it turned out, the conversation with Preston was a waste of time. The man had tricked Beanie with ridiculous lies. He expected nothing less from Zach Preston today.

"Good Morning, Mr. Preston," said Beanie, walking toward the chair closest to the man who'd been arrested for killing Gavin de Grac. The strange man looked the same as when Beanie first met him. Preston's sunburned face was lined with deep fissures that reminded Beanie of grooves carved into dusty leather. He wore a tropical shirt, opened to the third button, and his bleached hair looked like strands of frayed, knotted rope.

Preston gave him a curt nod and a shrewd stare.

Beanie pulled out a chair and took a seat. "How can I help you?"

"First of all," began Preston, "you need to know that I am an innocent man."

"Not according to Detective Janvier of the St. Killian Police Department."

Preston scoffed. "They got the wrong man. Again. I didn't kill anybody."

"The cops think you did. And the evidence against you is very compelling," said Beanie, recalling what Fields had told him. "The gun used to kill Gavin de Grac was found at your residence. Buried in your backyard. De Grac's blood was found on one of your shirts, also buried in your backyard."

"Wasn't my shirt," insisted Preston. "Cops showed it to me. Some kind of cricket shirt."

"Cricket shirt?"

"I don't even watch cricket," said Preston. "Never have. Don't understand that game."

A memory flared within Beanie. Cricket shirt? Why did that seem familiar? Had he seen someone wearing—

"I didn't bury those things in my backyard," thundered Preston, his eyes wild and furious. "I didn't kill anyone. I was set up. Framed."

"Framed?"

"By the men who wanted me dead," said Preston, trembling, his face florid.

"The men who wanted you dead?" Beanie shook his head. "Oh, you mean the three men you sent me on a wild goat chase to St. X to figure out which one was a murderer?"

Preston shook his head and said, "Wasn't a wild goat chase. One of those men—"

"None of those men knew what you were talking about," said Beanie. "They had never heard of Gavin de Grac. Never heard of you—"

"They were lying," said Preston, banging his fists on the table. "Of course, they weren't going to admit their crimes. You were supposed to trick them into confessing. I thought you were a competent reporter."

Taken aback by the man's insult, Beanie stood. "Okay, we're done here."

"No, wait, wait!" Preston held up his hands, his gaze pleading and panicked. "Please. I'm sorry. I didn't mean to speak negatively about your skills. It's just … I'm fighting for my freedom. For my life. I did not kill Gavin de Grac. The man saved my life."

Beanie sat down again. "He saved your life when he warned you that the three men had come to St. Killian to kill you."

Nodding, Preston said, "And then one of those three men killed him. And now, those men are trying to frame me. They didn't get a chance to take my life, so now they want to take my freedom."

Beanie sighed. "Okay, if you're telling the truth—"

"I swear that I am," insisted Preston.

"Then how do you explain the evidence buried in your backyard?"

"One of those men must have buried it," said Preston.

"Of course," said Beanie, not bothering to hide his sarcasm.

"I'm telling the truth," said Preston. "And I know who it was …"

"One of the three men?"

Preston exhaled and hung his head. "I don't know which of the men it was … and for all I know, all three had a hand in this treachery. But, the cops need to find out who sent them that so-called anonymous tip."

Beanie rubbed his jaw. Fields had told him that the police were tipped off about Zach Preston. Someone claiming to be one of Preston's neighbors said they'd seen him burying items in his backyard.

According to Fields, the neighbor didn't want to reveal her identity. She'd told the cops she feared Preston would retaliate and hurt her.

"What about the fact that you don't have an alibi for the night de Grac was killed?" asked Beanie.

"It's like I told the cops," said Preston. "The man who could give me an alibi is dead. I was with Gavin the night he was murdered."

"I'm sure you were," said Beanie, growing weary with the conversation. "The killer usually is with the victim when the killer kills the victim."

Preston dragged his hands down his craggy face. "Look, what I meant was … the night Gavin was killed, he had come to see me … to tell me the men planned to kill me. And then Gavin got a phone call, and he had to leave. That was the last time I saw him."

Beanie let out a frustrated breath. "Mr. Preston. I can't help you, okay?"

"But—"

"I can't help you because I don't believe you," said Beanie. "I believe Detective Janvier arrested the right man, and trust me, that's difficult for me to admit. The evidence shows that you're the killer. You were in possession of the gun used to kill Gavin de Grac. The victim's blood was on your clothing. And you just admitted to me that you were with the victim the night he died. I don't think Gavin was warning you about three men who wanted to kill you."

Shaking his head, Zach Preston looked away.

"I think you had some sort of beef with Gavin de Grac," said Beanie. "The two of you argued. And then both of you pulled out weapons on each other. And in the end, the bullets you fired hit their target. Gavin is dead because you killed him."

27

"So I was right about Gavin de Grac's secret girlfriend," said Caleb, arms crossed as he leaned back in his chair.

"I wouldn't call her a secret girlfriend," disputed Beanie, annoyed by Caleb's smug, satisfied look. "She was more like a casual hookup. But, yes … Trina Walters wanted Gavin dead because he wasn't going to leave his wife and marry her."

A week had passed since Beanie had written COPS ARREST SUSPECT IN DEATH OF MAN FOUND ON BEACH. Zach Preston, who claimed he was innocent, would remain out on bail until his trial.

"Trina Walters gave Tommy Mizell two thousand dollars to kill Gavin," began Beanie, looking at Stevie and then Caleb, who sat with him at a table in the *Palmchat Gazette* breakroom. "Then Trina planned to accuse Nora de Grac of taking out the hit."

"Crazy what people will do for love," remarked Stevie, unscrewing the cap on a bottle of water.

"Silly, fool girl," grumbled Caleb. "Did she really think that ridiculous plan would work?"

"Trina thought the insurance policy would convince the police that Nora had Gavin killed to collect three hundred thousand dollars," said

Beanie. "But Nora didn't take out the policy. Trina created the policy and forged Nora's signature."

"What was Trina going to do when Nora denied the accusations?" asked Stevie after a gulp of water.

"Didn't the silly fool girl know that any half-decent handwriting analysis expert would have been able to prove that the signature on the policy was forged?" asked Caleb.

Shaking his head, Beanie said, "I don't think she was thinking the whole situation through. Anyway, the cops kept ignoring Trina's allegations because Nora de Grac and Tommy Mizell had alibis for the night Gavin de Grac was murdered."

"How do you know?" asked Stevie, sipping more water.

"I had lunch with Fields earlier," said Beanie, taking a sip of his second cup of coffee of the day. "Janvier had cleared them weeks ago. He'd checked out Nora de Grac first because she was the wife."

"And those closest to the victim are always under suspicion," said Caleb, nodding.

Beanie said, "When Trina Walters accused Tommy Mizell of working with Nora, Janvier checked out the janitor and the secretary. Janvier also checked out Trina's claims about the insurance policy. Turns out, all policies are created by the insurance agents. When Janvier questioned the agents, neither of them had heard of Nora de Grac. But, when they searched their files for the policy, they discovered it on their computer system. The digital fingerprint traced back to Trina. She'd created the policy on her work computer during her lunch hour."

"Will Trina Walters face any charges for trying to have Gavin de Grac killed?" asked Stevie.

"I'm not sure," said Beanie. "Fields thinks it's unlikely because Mizell refuses to snitch on Trina, and Trina is now telling the police that she lied about the hit to get Nora in trouble."

Caleb let out a short, mirthless laugh. "The silly fool girl didn't bother to mention that *she* paid Mizell to kill Gavin."

"And Mizell is denying everything," said Beanie. "He's telling the cops that he doesn't know why Trina would put his name in her crazy plot."

Caleb said, "Well, at least Janvier got it right this time."

"Believe it or not," said Stevie.

Chuckling, Beanie stood. "And I actually believe it."

Moments later, as he walked back to his tiny cubicle, Beanie's cell phone rang. "Roland Bean," he answered, stepping into his cube.

"Yeah, this is Ferris," said the caller. "My coworker said you wanted me to give you a call."

Confused, Beanie said, "Your coworker?"

"I work at Swaying Palms Inn," the man said. "I'm one of the motel clerks. My coworker said you had some questions."

"Oh, yeah," said Beanie, remembering. "I did have questions, but—"

"About that dead man, right?" interrupted Ferris. "The one they found on Mango Beach. Him and his friends."

"His friends?"

"Three old dudes," said Ferris. "About the same age as him. Mid-to-late sixties. They was in town for a fishing trip. I think that's what they said."

"A fishing trip?"

"The three friends was from St. X," said Ferris. "The old dude that got killed told me he was from St. X, too, but he moved to St. Killian."

Beanie sank into his squeaky leather chair. "I'm sorry, Mr. Ferris. Who did you say was from St. X?"

"The old dead dude's friends," said Ferris. "The three friends came to St. Killian to fish with the dead guy. Some kind of old boys' trip, I guess."

"So, you're telling me that the man who was found dead stayed at the Swaying Palms with three of his friends?" asked Beanie, searching for clarity, even though he wasn't sure what he needed to be clear about.

"Well, no," said Ferris. "The three friends stayed at the motel. The dead guy just visited them during the day. Sometimes at night. But the dead guy never stayed overnight. He paid for the room, though. Twin beds plus extra for a rollaway bed. What was his name? Hold on, let me check the records."

In the ensuing silence, Beanie heard the tapping of computer keys.

The hypnotic staccato sent Beanie's mind wandering. And yet he wasn't sure what to think. Gavin de Grac had stayed at the Swaying Palms motel with three friends from St. Xavier. Beanie couldn't help thinking about Zach Preston. The gaunt, sunbaked man insisted that three men from St. Xavier had traveled to St. Killian to kill him. Preston claimed that Gavin de Grac had warned him about the men's nefarious plot.

Beanie hadn't believed him. Had been convinced Preston was a liar. First, he'd pegged Preston as an attention seeker who derived sick pleasure from providing fake leads. Then, after a gun and bloody clothes were found buried in Preston's backyard, Beanie realized the man was a cold-blooded killer.

But was that true?

"Gavin de Grac paid for the motel room," said Ferris. "That's the dead man, right? I remember that name from the paper. They arrested the man who killed him, right?"

Beanie cleared his throat. "Listen, Ferris … the friends who stayed in the motel room … what were their names?"

"Not sure about that," said Ferris. "This ain't the Queen Palm Resort & Spa. If guests don't want to give us their names, we don't worry about it. The guy that owns this place just wants the rates paid."

"What about surveillance cameras?" asked Beanie, hoping video footage might have caught images of the three friends. If Preston had been telling the truth about the trio from St. X, then Beanie figured he'd be able to recognize the men if the surveillance was clear enough.

"Again, this ain't the Queen Palm," said Ferris, chuckling. "No cameras. Too expensive. The owner looked into getting cameras a few years ago, but he didn't want to pay for the installation, monitoring, or maintenance."

"I was just wondering because I need to find out who those three men are," said Beanie.

"Yeah, I don't know," said Ferris. "Sorry, I can't help with that."

"No, I understand," said Beanie. "You've actually been very helpful …"

After ending the call with Ferris, Beanie leaned back in his chair. He wasn't sure if Ferris had been helpful or not. What exactly had the motel clerk done? Given him information about a trio of men who'd stayed at the motel in a room paid for by Gavin de Grac. What was helpful about that?

Beanie looked up at the ceiling tiles.

Did he need to know the names of the three men? Did he need to find out if the three men who'd stayed in the motel were the same men Preston said had traveled to St. Killian to kill him? Possibly. If Preston had been telling the truth about the three men, then … what?

Did that mean Preston hadn't killed Gavin de Grac? That he'd been framed by one of three men who'd initially wanted to kill him? Not necessarily. Preston might have been telling the truth about the identity of the three men. But he could have lied about the trio's reason for traveling to St. Killian.

Rubbing his jaw, Beanie sat forward. The men might have come to St. Killian to fish. Preston might have had a reason to target Gavin de Grac and the three men. Preston might have lured the men to St. Killian to kill them. Gavin might have been trying to protect the three men from Preston.

Beanie pinched the bridge of his nose.

Part of him wanted to move on from the murder of Gavin de Grac. A suspect had been arrested. The evidence against Zach Preston was compelling. Detective Janvier had closed the case.

But another part of him couldn't help wondering if he should make sure that the right person had been captured.

28

"This information is not free," said Ruben Fitzgerald. "Nor is it cheap."

With frustration and mild disgust, Beanie stared at the low-rent private investigator. From what Stevie had told him about the mercenary gumshoe, Beanie figured the information he needed would cost him. What he still didn't know was if he needed the information.

Following the conversation with Ferris, the Swaying Palms motel clerk, Beanie had conferred with his coworkers, Stevie and Caleb. Neither man was convinced that the motel clerk's information was substantial enough to warrant further investigation. Three men from St. X had stayed at a Little Turkey motel, but that didn't mean Zach Preston had been telling the truth. There was no proof that the men had traveled to St. Killian to kill Preston.

The men might have planned a fishing trip with Gavin de Grac. Preston might have known about the fishing trip. He could have been aware that the men were in St. Killian, and he might have decided to deflect suspicion on the trio.

Nevertheless, both Stevie and Caleb were interested and intrigued by the idea that three men from St. X seemed to have a connection to Gavin de Grac. But what was the connection? And who were the men?

Caleb and Stevie believed that Beanie needed to find out the names of the three men before investigating further.

If the three men from St. X turned out to be Archie Hall, Dennis Woodard, and Tarragon Ungaro, Beanie would decide whether or not looking deeper into things would be worth it or a waste of time.

In order to help make the decision, Beanie decided to contact Ruben Fitzgerald. He hoped the private investigator could tell him more about the manila folder found in room 729 at the Swaying Palms. Why were photos of Zach Preston inside the folder? Since Fitzgerald's business card was attached to the photos, Beanie wondered if the man had information about the pictures of Preston.

Because the folder had been recovered from the motel room occupied by the three men from St. X, Beanie wanted to know if the three men knew anything about the photos. Fitzgerald might be able to answer that question if he knew the men's identities. Of course, the private investigator would only know the men if they'd solicited his services. And if they had, then …

Beanie cautioned himself not to get ahead of things. First things first. Determine if Fitzgerald knew anything about the identity of the three men.

Fitzgerald delved his hand into a glass bowl of M&Ms on his desk and scooped out a handful. "I'm going to need three hundred bucks, or I'm not going to have anything to say."

Sighing, Beanie removed his wallet. The one hundred dollar bills he extracted didn't belong to him. The money had been taken from the *Palmchat Gazette*'s petty cash fund. Vivian had authorized payment of up to five hundred dollars after he explained why he wanted to speak with Fitzgerald. Having done business with the shady P.I., Vivian was aware of the man's unabashed greed.

After locking the money in one of his desk drawers, Fitzgerald leaned back in his chair and shoved the M&Ms into his mouth. "So, what do you want to know?"

Shifting in the uncomfortable chair opposite the desk, Beanie said,

"As I told you on the phone, I need information about the manila folder that contained photos of Zach Preston."

Chomping the candy, Fitzgerald scratched the side of his nose. "Zach Preston. He was arrested recently, right?"

Beanie nodded. "That's right."

"Why do you want to know about the photos of Preston?" asked Fitzgerald, his eyes narrowed.

"I want to know what you know about them," said Beanie, hoping the private investigator didn't want to engage in a cagey, back-and-forth conversation.

Fitzgerald grabbed another handful of M&Ms. "I took the photos of Zach Preston."

"Why?"

"I was paid to surveil the man," said Fitzgerald, "and get photos of him. Which I did, at the behest of my client."

Beanie asked, "And who was the client?"

Grinding the colorful candies between his stained teeth, Fitzgerald said, "Gavin de Grac."

29

"De Grac came to me about a month ago," said Fitzgerald, shoving more M&Ms in his mouth as he explained why Gavin de Grac wanted to hire him. "A woman named Lisa Roget had contacted de Grac about a man named Zachary Preston. de Grac wanted me to determine if Zachary Preston was still alive."

"de Grac thought Preston was dead?"

"Apparently, de Grac had been told, ten years ago, that Preston was killed in a car accident," said Fitzgerald. "Ironically, Lisa Roget told de Grac that Preston died. According to de Grac, ten years ago, Lisa Roget sent him a newspaper article. De Grac gave me a copy. I have it right here … "

Beanie stared at the photocopy of the article, which had appeared in *The Cotswold Times*, a weekly newspaper published in Cotswold, England.

The man, identified as Zachary Preston by his partner, Lisa Ann Roget, had lost control of the car during severely inclement weather. Roget, in the passenger seat, escaped the vehicle after it slammed into a tree. Roget was trying to extract Mr. Preston when the car caught fire. Mr. Preston's burned body was recovered.

The news story had an accompanying photo.

Beanie stared at the picture of the man. The hair was neatly groomed and cut in a close-cropped style. The lines and grooves on the face were not so severe. Still, it was clearly Zachary Preston.

Beanie didn't understand.

Fitzgerald said, "Neither did I. But I wasn't paid to figure it out. All de Grac wanted me to do was determine if Lisa Roget was telling him the truth. I figured the best way to do that would be to follow her. And sure enough, she led me to Zach Preston. At that point, I started following Preston. Got several photos of him, which I put in the manila folder and delivered to de Grac.

"Did you take the folder to the Swaying Palms motel?"

Fitzgerald shook his head. "Took the file to de Grac's house. Gave him the file. Got my money. And that was it."

"Did de Grac tell you what he was going to do with the photos?"

"Didn't ask. Didn't really care," said Fitzgerald. "But I figured de Grac was going to confront Preston. I'm assuming that happened because Preston shot and killed de Grac."

"Yeah, he did," confirmed Beanie.

"I'm not surprised," said Fitzgerald. "Preston was a tough old dude. This one time, I was following him, and he made me. Grabbed me and roughed me up. Demanded to know why I was following him."

"Did you tell him?"

"You bet I did," said Fitzgerald. "And Preston gave me a warning."

"Told you to stop following him?" guessed Beanie.

"The warning was for Gavin de Grac," said Fitzgerald. "Preston said, you tell de Grac to stay away from me, or I'll kill him … "

30

"So, now do you believe that Janvier was right about Zach Preston killing Gavin de Grac?"

Beanie took a sip of beer and glanced at Officer Fields. Although, this evening, in Beanie's backyard, Officer Fields was simply Damon, a good friend who'd accepted an invitation to enjoy grilled goat burgers with Beanie, Noelle, and Noelle's new bestie, Amber.

A few days ago, during breakfast with Fields, Beanie had casually mentioned that Noelle wanted to introduce him to one of her friends.

"Simple backyard barbeque," Beanie had said as he and Fields left the small café. "Nothing fancy. And if you're going to be busy, it's no problem—"

"I'm not going to be busy," Fields had cut in.

"How do you know you won't be busy?" asked Beanie, shocked by the eagerness in the officer's tone.

"Because I won't be busy," said Fields. "Text me the details, and I'll be there."

And Fields was here.

Two hours early.

The officer, who looked rather dapper in light-colored trousers and an aqua polo, claimed he'd overestimated how much traffic he'd face traveling from his apartment to Oyster Farms. In reality, it only took about forty-five minutes from Field's neighborhood to Beanie's modest home in the well-kept working-class enclave. Beanie had a feeling—one his wife shared—that Fields was nervous. The man had opened three Felipe beers but had yet to finish one. He would nurse the island brew until it became too warm to drink, thus forcing him to pop the top on another one.

Beanie decided to calm Fields down by discussing the Gavin de Grac murder case.

Stoking the charcoal in the small grill, Beanie said, "I will confess that for a minute or two, I wondered if Preston had actually told me the truth."

"You thought three guys had come to St. Killian to kill him?"

Beanie sat his half-empty beer bottle on the tray attached to the grill. "When I found out de Grac had paid for three men to stay at the Swaying Palms, I was thinking … why? I was thinking, had those three men come to hurt Preston?"

"But Preston told you de Grac warned him about the three guys, right?" asked Fields. "So, why would de Grac pay for three men to stay at a motel where they plotted to kill Preston but then turn around and tell Preston about the plot. Doesn't make sense."

"No, it doesn't," said Beanie, wiping his brow as smoky heat from the grill wafted toward his face. "I didn't even think of that, but now that you've said it."

"The private investigator's story convinces me that Preston did it," said Fields.

Beanie used a long-handled fork to move the coals around. "Preston and de Grac must have had some sort of beef."

"Can you imagine thinking the guy you had beef with was dead?" Fields shook his head. "And then you find out he's alive."

"You know, I'm starting to wonder if de Grac planned to confront Preston," said Beanie. "Maybe de Grac just wanted to know that Preston was still alive. But, then Preston found out that de Grac was having him followed."

"You think Preston confronted de Grac?"

"Preston told Fitzgerald he would kill de Grac," said Beanie. "Maybe de Grac wanted to settle the beef, but Preston decided to end it for good."

Fields shook his head. "I actually think de Grac was the aggressor. Remember, he took Stanley Iris' gun. I think de Grac took the gun to threaten Preston. The two old guys had a shootout, and Preston won."

"And then made up a story about three men coming to kill him, but then they killed de Grac because he warned Preston about their plan."

"Preston is a liar," said Fields, taking a sip of beer. "The man faked his death. Had his girlfriend—"

"I don't know if Lisa Roget is Preston's girlfriend," interjected Beanie.

"Whatever she is to him doesn't matter," said Fields. "The point is, Lisa Roget sent de Grac the article about Preston's death. I'll bet Preston told her to do that."

"That's what I want to find out," said Beanie. "Did Preston want de Grac to think he was dead? If so, why? What's the connection between de Grac and Preston? The real connection. Not that lie Preston told me about de Grac warning him that three men were planning to kill him. Preston wouldn't even tell me how he knew de Grac."

"And you think Lisa Roget will?"

"I'm hoping," said Beanie. "She might be able to provide the last pieces of this weird puzzle."

"What weird puzzle?" Noelle's voice rang out behind Beanie.

Turning from the grill, Beanie smiled as his wife strolled toward him, looking fetching and lovely in a sleeveless lavender sundress.

"The connection between Zach Preston and Gavin de Grac," answered Fields.

"Figure that out later," said Noelle. "Is the grill ready? We should get the burgers on now."

"About five minutes," said Beanie.

Noelle said, "Perfect. Amber will be here in five minutes."

"She will?" asked Fields.

Staring at Fields' shell-shocked expression, Beanie held in a laugh.

Nodding, Noelle said, "Come with me."

As Noelle strode back toward the house, Fields turned to Beanie.

"Relax, man," said Beanie.

Fields nodded, but his Adam's apple bobbed. "Easy for you to say. You don't have to impress a beautiful woman."

"And neither do you," said Beanie. "Just be yourself."

Fields groaned. "Before I go … do I look okay?"

31

"All I know is that Gavin and Zach had some kind of beef," said Lisa Roget, stocking candles shaped like seashells on a shelf at the back of the small store, which was empty and would close in an hour.

Beanie had obtained the woman's contact information from Ruben Fitzgerald. He'd called her the day before and left a message, which he hadn't expected her to return. Much to his surprise, when he'd arrived at the *Palmchat Gazette* that morning, the message from Lisa Roget, returning his call, had been the first voice mail.

After lunch with Stevie, Beanie had reached Lisa Roget, and they'd agreed to meet later that evening at her job, a small souvenir shop near the ferry station.

"And Zach told you to send Gavin the news article that said he'd died in a car accident?" asked Beanie.

Nodding, Lisa removed another candle from the cardboard box sitting on a stool. "Told me it was best if Gavin thought he was dead."

"And he didn't tell you why?"

Lisa shook her head. "Zach wasn't the kind of guy who liked to explain his actions. And to tell you the truth, I was still trying to process why he'd faked his death in the first place."

"Tell me more about that," requested Beanie.

Staring at the candle she held, Lisa said, "This all happened ten years ago after me and Zach left the Palmchat Islands. We moved to Cotswold. The English countryside. Anyway, me, Zach, and a friend of Zach's were driving during a thunderstorm. The friend's name was Pete. Pete was driving, and he lost control of the car. Slammed into a tree. Me and Zach got out. The car caught fire and blew up before we could get Pete out. As I watched the car burn, I was in shock. Not quite sure what to do. Couldn't believe what had just happened. And then Zach told me to tell the cops that he was driving, and not to mention our friend."

"And you told the cops that?"

Lisa placed the candle on the shelf, making room for it between the other candles. "Back then, I did whatever Zach said. No questions asked. Well, no, I asked questions. But if Zack didn't answer them, I didn't push it. Guess that's how much in love I was with him. Anyway, before the cops and the ambulance showed up, Zach took off. He told me he would explain later, but he never did. Just said it was better off if people thought he was dead."

"And Pete's family never wondered what happened to him?"

"I don't think Pete had any family," said Lisa, reaching into the box for another candle. "Not that I know of, anyway. I think that's how Zach was able to impersonate Pete for a while."

"Zach stole Pete's identity?"

Lisa nodded. "Until me and him came back to the Palmchat Islands."

Confused, Beanie said, "So let me get this straight: You and Zach were together for the entire ten years between the time when he faked his death and when the two of you came back to the Palmchat Islands?"

Nodding her head, Lisa said, "That's right."

Seeking further clarification, Beanie asked, "You spent the past ten years with a man who was pretending to be someone else?"

Shrugging, Lisa said, "Well, yeah, but …"

"But?"

"Zach only pretended to be Pete in official situations, you know?"

Lisa moved the candles to make room for more candles. "Like, if he needed to apply for a job or open a bank account."

"And no one ever discovered that Zach was using the identity of a dead man?"

"Sometimes somebody would get suspicious," said Lisa. "But, then me, and Zach would move to another small town or village where no one knew us."

"If Zach wanted people to think he was dead, why did he come back to the Palmchat Islands?" asked Beanie, reflecting on the strange situation, which, he supposed, explained why he'd run into a dead-end during his search of Zach Preston's background.

"He never really did say," said Lisa, tilting her head as though this was the first time she'd contemplated the question. "All I can think is this was his home, and he missed it."

"So, he came back to St. Killian as Zach Preston?" asked Beanie.

"We came back last year," said Lisa.

"Did anyone ask him about coming back from the dead?"

Lisa glanced at him. "Now that I think about it, he didn't tell me to send that article to anyone else other than Gavin de Grac. And Zach didn't have any family either. Both his parents died when he was a teenager. They were originally from Canada. Came here on their honeymoon, fell in love with the island, and stayed. Zach's relatives are all in Ontario, but he never had much contact with them."

Beanie asked, "So why did you contact Gavin and tell him that Zach was alive?"

Shrugging, Lisa said, "Revenge."

"Revenge?"

"Found out Zach had cheated on me," said Lisa, making room on the shelf for yet another candle. "Actually, had been cheating on me for a long time with lots of different women. He claimed they didn't mean anything to him, of course."

"So you wanted to get back at Zach?"

Lisa sighed. "I didn't think Zach would kill Gavin. If anything, I thought Gavin would kill Zach. One of the things Zach had told me was that Gavin saw him as an enemy. This was ten years ago when I asked Zach why he wanted Gavin to think he was dead. And Zach said that Gavin would be glad that he was dead and would want him to rot in hell. So, when I found out about all the other women, I guess I was thinking ... "

"Thinking what?"

Exhaling, Lisa said, "I wanted to kill Zach for making a fool of me. But I knew I couldn't do it because I'm stupid, and I still love him, but maybe Gavin de Grac ... "

Beanie said, "You thought that if you told Gavin that Zach was alive, then Gavin would go after Zach and kill him?"

Lisa shook her head as a small, sad laugh escaped her lips. "But it didn't work like that. Revenge never does. I wanted a man dead. But the wrong man was killed."

32

"Mr. Bean, it's Ferris …"

"Ferris …?" Beanie frowned, trying to remember if he knew the name, and if so, from where or why.

"From the Swaying Palms motel. You called me last week about the three old guys who stayed in room 729."

"Oh, yeah, right. Right." Wondering why the man was calling, Beanie cleared his throat. "How are you?"

"Wanted to tell you I found out the names of those three guys," said Ferris. "When we spoke, I forgot to tell you that my cousin—he's an independent cab driver—drove the guys around town the week they were here."

"Oh, well—"

"My cousin gave me their names," said Ferris. "He got to know the guys. I wrote down the names. Let's see. We got … Archie Hall. Dennis … something … can't read my own handwriting. Dennis Woodard, and—"

"Wait, what?" Beanie cut in. "What was the first name?"

"Archie Hall," said Ferris. "And then Dennis Woodard. And …

Tarragon Ungaro. Tarragon. Ha! Never heard that name before. Interesting. Didn't expect that."

"Yeah," said Beanie, rubbing his jaw. "Neither did I …"

"Was there something you needed to know about those three guys?" asked Ferris. "My cousin would probably be able to tell you. Like I said, he drove them around when they were in town."

"Yeah …" said Beanie. "I think I would like to talk to your cousin."

Later that afternoon, sitting at a table in the breakroom with his coworkers Caleb and Stevie, Beanie asked, "So what do you think?"

"Question is, what do you think?" asked Caleb.

Shaking his head, Beanie said, "I don't know what to think. That's why I wanted to see what you guys think. I mean, Preston told the truth about Archie, Dennis, and Tarragon. They came to St. Killian. They stayed a week at the Swaying Palms motel."

"Yeah, but you don't know why," said Stevie.

"Exactly," agreed Caleb. "Preston told the truth about the three men traveling to St. Killian. But did they come here to kill him?"

"Maybe that's why you should talk to Ferris's cousin," said Stevie.

"But what can the cousin tell me about the three men?" asked Beanie. "If they did come to St. Killian to kill Preston, I doubt they admitted that to the cousin."

"They would have lied to a cab driver about the reason for their visit," said Caleb.

"Right," said Beanie. "Probably told the cab driver what they told Ferris. They were in town for a fishing trip."

Stevie took a sip of water, then said, "Well, you know they lied to you."

Nodding, Caleb said, "All three of the men denied any recent trips to St. Killian."

"And don't forget," said Stevie, "they both told you they didn't know Gavin de Grac."

"Another lie," said Caleb. "De Grac paid for those men to stay at the Swaying Palms. You really think they didn't know him?"

"Obviously, they didn't want anyone to know they knew Gavin," said

Stevie, taking another sip of water. "But why? Maybe because Gavin was killed. Maybe they didn't want to be questioned about his murder. They didn't want to be asked if they knew who wanted to kill him. Because maybe they wanted him dead."

Beanie shook his head. "I still think Preston killed de Grac. The murder weapon was found in his backyard. He had beef with de Grac. He has no alibi for the night de Grac was killed."

Caleb said, "Those three men are obviously hiding something. They know more about de Grac's murder than they're telling."

"I wonder if they know Preston killed de Grac," said Stevie, "but they're not saying anything because they're afraid of Preston. Maybe they don't want to end up like Gavin de Grac."

"But I don't even know if those three guys know Preston," said Beanie.

"Well, you know they were in the motel room where you found the photos of Preston," said Stevie. "Gavin had to have left the photos in that room. Maybe he showed the photos of Preston to the three guys."

"But why?" asked Beanie.

"Find out. Do they have some connection to Preston? Why were they in St. Killian?" asked Caleb. "And why did they lie about being on the island and knowing de Grac."

33

"I remember thinking, yeah, they're in St. Killian to fish, alright," said Ferris's cousin, Jared, sitting on the trunk of his dark blue mid-sized sedan.

The roar of an airplane taking off arrested Beanie's attention for a moment. Earlier that morning, Beanie called Jared and agreed to meet the man at the St. Killian International Airport.

Catching the derisiveness in the man's chuckle, Beanie said nothing and waited for Jared to continue.

Following his conversation with Stevie and Caleb yesterday, Beanie had spent the remainder of the evening wondering if Zach Preston had murdered Gavin de Grac. By morning, he felt even more compelled to determine whether or not Janvier had arrested the right man.

He wanted to make certain that Preston was lying about the three men from St. X. It was true that they'd visited St. Killian, but why? To fish? Or to kill Preston? And what exactly was their connection to de Grac? Why had the dead man paid for the trio to stay at the seedy Swaying Palms motel? And why had the men lied about traveling to St. Killian? Why had they all pretended they'd never heard of Gavin de Grac?

"But they're not fishing for fish. You know what I mean?"

"I'm not sure I do," said Beanie.

"It's like this," began Jared. "Something was … I don't know … kind of off about them."

"What do you mean?" asked Beanie. "Off how?"

"Seemed like they were always stressed," said Jared. "Always tense. I mean, they're supposed to be in town for a fishing trip. Supposed to be friends getting together to relax and have a good time. But, they were always frowning. Never smiling. Never laughing. Always looked like they were going to a funeral."

"Did you ask them about their bad mood?"

Jared shrugged. "I tried to hold a conversation. Tried to be cordial. Make jokes. They just wanted me to shut up and drive. So I did."

"Where did you drive them?"

Exhaling, Jared said, "Let's see … a couple of mornings, I drove them to breakfast. Café right around from the motel. Then in the afternoons, they'd call me, and I would pick them up, drive them to get something to eat."

"Where'd they go for dinner?" asked Beanie.

"Mostly, we stopped at food stands on the side of the road," said Jared. "But one night, I took them to Dizzy Jenny's."

Beanie made a note of that particular detail in his notetaking app. The newspaper had a source at Dizzy Jenny's, a popular upscale beachfront restaurant. Landon George, the source, wasn't always cooperative. But Beanie hoped the bartender might tell him if he recognized the three men from their Palmchat Island driver's license photos. Jared said, "Then, a few hours later, I'd pick them up and take them back to the motel. What they did after that, I don't know … except for one night when I drove them to this house in Seashell Estates."

"Do you know who they were visiting?" asked Beanie.

Jared shook his head. "Nobody, as far as I know."

"What do you mean?"

"They didn't get out of the car," said Jared. "Just wanted me to drive by the house a few times."

"Why?"

"No idea," said Jared. "But, it felt like they were casing the joint, you know? They said they were looking for an old friend's house, but they weren't sure if that was the house or not. That's why they wanted me to drive by a few times. But then they weren't sure, so they told me to take them back to the hotel."

"I wonder who the old friend was," said Beanie.

"Maybe you can find out," said Jared. "The address is still in my GPS log if you want it …"

Beanie nodded. "Yeah, I would …"

Jumping off the trunk, Jared walked to the driver's door, opened it, and got in the car. As the cab driver fiddled with the GPS, Beanie stared toward the line of cabs stretched along the curb. Whose house had the men wanted Jared to drive by? And why? Could the story the trio had given Jared be true? Had they been trying to determine if the house belonged to an old friend? Or were they casing the house, as Jared suspected? But if they had been, why?

The driver's door slammed, startling Beanie from his thoughts.

Jared walked toward him. "I wrote the address on the back of one of my business cards."

"Thanks." Beanie took the 2 x 3 card.

"Listen, there's something else I guess I should tell you …"

"What's that?"

"I don't know if it matters, but …" Jared looked away for a second, then back toward Beanie. "One of the old guys had an interesting request."

"Interesting request?"

Frowning, Jared said, "He asked me if I knew where he could get a gun. One that couldn't be traced."

"Why did he need an untraceable gun?"

"Protection, he claimed."

"Protection from what?" asked Beanie. "From who?"

"Said he'd heard Little Turkey was dangerous," said Jared.

"Which one of them men asked for the gun?" Beanie asked.

"The nice one," said Jared. "Mr. Dennis. He was the only one interested in talking. He would say good morning when I greeted him. He would engage in conversation. He wasn't super friendly, but he wasn't rude, you know?"

Beanie asked, "Did you—"

"Help him find a gun?" asked Jared, his tone and expression laced with offense. "No way. Especially since I didn't believe him. I mean, they're supposed to be in St. Killian to fish, right? So, what does the old dude need a gun for?"

34

Two hours later, after stopping at Pourciau Square for lunch at the Loco Goat food truck, Beanie was back at the *Palmchat Gazette* offices.

Sitting at the small desk in his tiny cubicle, Beanie took a sip of his second cup of coffee of the day. Jared's question still floated in his mind, demanding an answer. What does the old dude need a gun for? Beanie had no idea. Only speculation. And even his conjecture felt flawed, as it was based on a premise he couldn't prove. A premise that didn't make sense. That he didn't believe.

Still, he entertained the thought that the old man—Mr. Dennis, the nice one—had wanted the gun because he planned to shoot Gavin de Grac. But, if that was true, Beanie would have to concede that Zach Preston had told him the truth. He'd have to believe the three old men had traveled to St. Killian to kill Preston. But Gavin de Grac had prevented Preston's murder. So, Dennis Woodard killed him.

Exhaling, Beanie leaned back in his squeaky leather chair.

There were problems with entertaining the theory of Woodard as de Grac's killer.

First of all, Beanie believed that Janvier had arrested the right suspect—Zach Preston. The murder weapon and clothes stained with de Grac's blood had been found buried in Preston's backyard. Preston had no alibi. And according to Lisa Roget, Preston and de Grac had a long-standing beef. Beanie couldn't forget that Preston was an accomplished liar. A man who'd used the tragic death of a friend to fake his own demise.

Second, there was no proof of any connection between the three men and Zach Preston. As Caleb had pointed out, or maybe it had been Stevie, the trio had lied about visiting St. Killian. But that didn't mean Preston had told the truth about the men wanting him dead.

Third, Beanie wondered if Dennis had tried to procure a gun for Gavin de Grac. Maybe the men had come to St. Killian to help de Grac confront Preston. Beanie doubted it, but he supposed it was possible.

Reaching into the pocket of his trousers, Beanie pulled out Jared's business card. Turning it over, he stared at the address scrawled on the back. According to the cab driver, he'd driven Archie Hall, Tarragon Ungaro, and Dennis Woodard to that residence.

Beanie turned to his computer. With a few clicks of his mouse, he accessed a property database that would allow him to enter the address and find out who owned the home. Seconds later, he gaped at the screen in disbelief.

The house, located in Seashell Estates, belonged to Zach Preston.

Exhaling a shaky breath, Beanie tried to marshal his scattered thoughts. Did the fact that the three men had directed the cab driver to take them to Preston's home mean they'd traveled to St. Killian to kill him? Beanie wasn't sure. But why would the three old guys have Preston's address? Why would they want to be driven past his home? Again, he wasn't sure.

What he did know was that the men had told him another lie. Well, Tarragon and Dennis had told a second lie when they'd denied knowing Zach Preston. Beanie was sure that if he'd had an opportunity to speak with Archie Hall, the man would have given him the same dishonest denials.

Rubbing his jaw, Beanie considered that the three men might not have known the address was to a house that belonged to Zach Preston. That was possible. But was it probable?

The desk phone rang.

"Roland Bean," said Beanie.

"Hey, it's Fields," said the affable officer. "I don't have long to talk but figured you'd want to know the latest regarding the de Grac murder case."

Beanie grabbed his mouse and made a few clicks, opening a Word document. "What's happened?" He asked, feeling a strange panic burst within him. His first thought was that Janvier had found evidence that disputed Zach Preston's guilt. Some clue that pointed to another suspect.

"So, Preston's attorney has challenged the collection of the evidence against his client," said Fields.

"Really?" Beanie was taken aback. "Why? I mean, the murder weapon was found in Preston's backyard."

"Well, the attorney is not disputing that," said Fields. "He's claiming that Preston is not the person who buried the gun in the backyard."

"That's not surprising," said Beanie, typing notes into the document.

"No, but it is odd that he's questioning the veracity and sincerity of the anonymous tip Janvier received, which led him to search Preston's backyard."

"Does the attorney think the anonymous tip was ... what? Faked or something?"

"Preston and his attorney allege the call was made by the person who planted the evidence at Preston's residence," said Fields. "They believe the real killer framed Preston by burying the gun and then called in the anonymous tip. The attorney wants the call traced. Janvier had already done that, though."

"Janvier knows the identity of the anonymous tipster?"

"Not the identity of the caller," said Fields. "But he knows the location of the call. Came from St. X."

The shock of panic gripped Beanie a second time. "St. X?"

"The anonymous tipster was calling from the St. Xavier Post Office ..."

35

"My lawyer doesn't want me talking to you," said Zach Preston.

"Then why are you talking to me?" asked Beanie, taking a seat across from Preston at the large, long oblong table in the *Palmchat Gazette*'s conference room.

Two days ago, Beanie had spoken with Officer Fields about the anonymous tipster's ties to St. Xavier. The information left Beanie feeling suspicious and unmoored. Immediately, Beanie recalled what he'd learned about Dennis Woodard from his research. Dennis was a mail carrier for the St. Xavier Postal Office.

Not only that, but Dennis had asked Jared to help him get a gun.

Beanie hadn't been sure what to think.

But he wondered if the attorney's theory was right. Had the real killer framed Preston and then called in a tip so the cops would be compelled to search Preston's backyard? Could Dennis be the real killer? If so, what was the man's motive? Beanie's investigation of the three men thus far had yielded no connection to Zach Preston.

"Something in your voice in that message you left me," began Preston, "made me think you might have some different thoughts about my story."

"Is that right?" asked Beanie.

Preston gave him a piercing stare. "Maybe you believe me now. Maybe you got a feeling that I've been telling you the truth all along."

Beanie took a deep breath. "Tell me about your beef with Gavin de Grac."

Frowning, Preston said, "That was a long time ago—"

"Ten years ago, right? You tricked de Grac into thinking you were dead," said Beanie. "Why did you tell Lisa Roget to send de Grac that newspaper article about you dying in a car accident?"

Preston scoffed. "You talked to Lisa, huh? Did you ask her why she went behind my back and told de Grac that I was alive?"

"She felt she had a good reason," said Beanie.

"I made a mistake," Preston said through clenched teeth. "I told her I was sorry."

"I don't think she believed you," said Beanie. "And maybe she was tired of lying for you."

"She was trying to get back at me."

Beanie shrugged. "Well, that's what happens when you cheat on people. Sometimes, they want to get you back for hurting them."

Preston looked away.

Beanie said, "Tell me about the beef with de Grac. Tell me why those three men want you dead. If you want me to believe you, then I need to know the truth."

"The beef between me and Gavin was over," said Preston. "We talked about things. Gavin said he wanted to bury the hatchet."

"And you believed him?"

Nodding, Preston said, "Gavin told me that he was trying to be a different person. A better man. He didn't have time to hold on to past hurts and offenses. He didn't want to dwell on things he couldn't change."

"You believed him?"

"The beef was over," insisted Preston. "It no longer mattered. Not to Gavin, at least. And I knew it was true because he warned me. He told me that Archie, Dennis, and Tarragon were coming after me."

"When did he tell you that?"

"The night he was killed," said Preston. "We met at my place in Mango Cove. Got a little beach shack out there that I rent out for extra income. Gavin and I met there. He told me that Archie, Tarragon, and Dennis were going to kill me. They'd come to St. Xavier to blow my head off."

"And yet Gavin ended up dead," said Beanie.

Preston banged a fist against the table. "Not by my hand. I did not kill Gavin. It was one of those three men."

"Which one?" demanded Beanie.

"I don't know," said Preston, dropping his head in his hands. "I wish I did."

Beanie pinched the bridge of his nose. "Okay, tell me this: why do Dennis, Archie, and Tarragon want to kill you?"

"Those men have a good reason for wanting me dead," said Preston. "After what I did to them, maybe I don't deserve to live ..."

36

Beanie wasn't sure he believed Zach Preston's story.

A few days had passed since the main suspect in the murder of Gavin de Grac had spoken to him for the third time in the *Palmchat Gazette* conference room.

During their meeting, Preston had come clean about why Archie, Dennis, and Tarragon wanted him dead.

A reason Beanie still found ... not quite compelling enough to inspire homicidal rage.

Driving home from a long, uneventful day at the paper, Beanie gripped the steering wheel of his SUV. Some days were slow news. Others, like today, were pretty much no news. At least, nothing exciting or intriguing. Beanie had spent most of the morning at the City Government Office, trying to stay awake as he listened to the mayor outline a new plan to encourage foreign business investment.

Following that, his afternoon lunch plans were interrupted by a tragic car accident on the island's west side. Only one vehicle had been involved in the horrific crash. Sadly, the driver, still unidentified, was killed when the car burst into flames.

As he navigated the traffic circle in the center of downtown St. Killian, Beanie thought about his last conversation with Zach Preston.

Those men have a good reason for wanting me dead. After what I did to them, maybe I don't deserve to live.

Preston had been unnecessarily melodramatic. He'd shared the man's confession with Caleb, Stevie, and Noelle. They all agreed with Beanie's assessment that what Preston had done was horrible but not necessarily heinous.

"I stole money from those men," Preston had said, hanging his head. "Convinced them to invest in worthless bonds. None of them had much money, to begin with, and I took what little they had, then high-tailed it out of town."

"And this was when?"

"Ten years ago."

"And how much money did you steal?"

"About five thousand from each man."

"Including Gavin?"

Preston nodded. "Him too."

"But Gavin forgave you?"

"Chalked it up as a lesson learned," said Preston. "Said it wouldn't have happened if he hadn't been greedy. Said he should have known my offer was too good to be true."

"But the other men didn't feel the same way?"

Preston said, "Gavin said they were determined to get their revenge. Make me pay."

"By killing you?"

Preston had nodded.

"Over fifteen thousand dollars?" Beanie had been skeptical that such a small amount of money could have warranted murder, but on the other hand, Archie Hall, Tarragon Ungaro, and Dennis Woodward were economically disadvantaged Palmchatters. They lived marginalized, meager lives in low-income neighborhoods.

Beanie imagined that each man might have given Zach Preston all the money they possessed. Preston's scam had probably wiped each man out. The trio had probably never recovered from such an economic disaster. Beanie had wrapped up the conversation. Thanked the man for his time. Once Preston was gone, Beanie felt, as he normally did after a conversation with the man, that he'd been duped. Preston's story felt incomplete. The man was a liar, so Beanie figured there was something he'd kept hidden. Question was, were Preston's secrets worth uncovering? Would a deeper investigation into Preston's story reveal a new suspect in the murder of Gavin de Grac? Or would Beanie confirm his belief that Preston was the killer?

Beanie's cell phone rang. Noelle's mom, he figured, even though he couldn't check the Caller-ID. The dashboard clock read 6:17 p.m. Normally, he picked up Ethan and Evan from their granny's house in Handweg around six o'clock.

Activating the Bluetooth option, Beanie said, "Sorry I'm running a little late, but—"

"Mr. Bean …?"

Beanie frowned. "Who is this?"

"Zach Preston."

Groaning inwardly, Beanie said, "Mr. Preston, I don't think—"

"I know who killed Gavin de Grac," said Preston.

"Okay, have you called the police?" asked Beanie, skeptical of the man's claims, wary of being fooled again.

"It was Dennis Woodard."

"Dennis?" asked Beanie. "Are you sure?"

"Positive," said Preston. "I have proof. I … shoot …"

"What is it?"

"Another call is coming through," said Preston. "I have to take it. Listen, if you want to talk—"

"Where are you now?"

"At home," said Preston. "Mr. Bean, I gotta go. I need to—"

"Listen, I'll stop by so we can talk," said Beanie. "I'm on my way …"

37

Thirty minutes later, Beanie turned into the neighborhood of Seashell Estates.

Much like Oyster Farms, his neighborhood, Seashell Estates, was populated with modest shotgun homes with small, well-kept lawns. After turning into the narrow driveway of Zach Preston's home, Beanie cut the engine. With a sigh, he stared toward the small porch.

Following his promise to visit Preston, Beanie called his mother-in-law Natalie to ask if she'd watch the boys a bit longer. His sons' grandmother didn't mind. She was more than happy. Natalie was always looking for ways to spend more time with her grandsons, especially since her relationship with Noelle was strained due to their disagreement about Noelle's father, Josue.

Beanie opened the door and exited the SUV. Initially, when Preston claimed that Dennis Woodard had killed Gavin de Grac, Beanie thought the man might be telling the truth. After all, Dennis had wanted a gun, according to Jared. But was there any other proof that the man was a murderer? The anonymous tip against Preston had been placed from a phone at the St. Xavier Postal Department. And Dennis worked there as a mail carrier. But that was hardly confirmation of Preston's belief that the real killer had framed him, then snitched to the police.

Then again, Beanie recalled his conversation with Dennis Woodard. The man had been very interested in the murder of Gavin de Grac. He'd asked lots of questions. Wanted lots of details. At the time, Beanie had pegged him as a nosy old man who watched too many true crime docuseries. But maybe Dennis had been trying to find out if the cops suspected him.

Beanie walked to the front door. The sun had set moments ago, but despite the residual light, the porch was dim and gloomy. Pressing a finger against the doorbell, Beanie waited.

A minute or so passed.

As a gust of balmy wind blew past Beanie's face, he exhaled and rang the doorbell again. Where was Preston? The man had just called him. Told Beanie he was home. Could he have left his house? Why would he have done that? Beanie had told the man he was planning to stop by.

Ignoring his annoyance, Beanie knocked on the door. "Mr. Preston? It's Roland Bean."

Behind him, a car drove by, and Beanie glanced over his shoulder.

The door opened.

Turning his head forward, Beanie stared at Zach Preston.

"Mr. Bean …"

"I told you I was coming over," said Beanie. "You remember?"

Preston stumbled over the threshold and onto the porch.

"Mr. Preston …" Side-stepping away from the swaying man, Beanie held his arms out as Preston lurched toward him. Beanie wondered if the man was drunk. Or maybe sick. Some kind of heart issue, possibly. "Are you okay?"

Shaking his head, his face sweaty and ashen, Zach Preston said, "He got me … that rascal got me …"

"What are you talking about?"

Grunting, Preston shuffled back into the house and under the light cast down from the overhead dome light.

At once, Beanie saw the sticky-looking red stain smeared across the misshapen, faded T-shirt hanging from Preston's bony frame.

"Mr. Preston, what happened?" Beanie put an arm around the man.

"Shot … me … "

"Who shot you?" asked Beanie, guiding the man into the living room. "Was it Dennis Woodard?"

"Didn't think he would … get me …" wheezed Preston, his chest heaving, eyes unfocused. "But … that rascal … tried to explain … "

"Mr. Preston, don't talk, okay?" Beanie stood. Shoving a trembling hand into his front pocket, he pulled out his phone. "I'm going to call 911."

"Never meant to … made mistakes …" Preston let out a whispery wail. "Maybe this is what … I deserve …"

38

"Mr. Bean, once again, you've found another dead body."

Beanie glared at Detective Philippi Janvier as the man strode toward him.

An hour had passed since his frantic, panicked 911 call. Fifteen minutes later, sirens blared. The next thing Beanie knew, the little shotgun house swarmed with cops and paramedics. As the police took his statement, the EMS team tried to revive Zach Preston, but the man succumbed to his injuries.

"Is that your thing? How do you manage it?" asked Janvier.

Beanie looked away from the detective's shrewd, suspicious look. But his gaze fell on the rug where Zach Preston died.

"Why is it that you're always around when someone drops dead?" inquired Janvier. "You remind me of a character on one of those silly television shows … the amateur sleuth is always tripping over a dead body."

Beanie resisted the urge to slug the man. "You want to take my statement here or at the station?"

"I will need an official statement, which I shall prefer to take place at the station," said Janvier. "But, tell me, what happened?"

Beanie recounted the events as he'd experienced them with clarity and dispassion.

The following morning, in the breakroom of the *Palmchat Gazette* offices, he told the same story to Caleb and Stevie but with a bit more enthusiasm.

Unscrewing the cap on the bottle of water he'd snagged from the refrigerator, Stevie asked, "So, did Preston kill de Grac or not? I'm a bit confused."

Beanie took a sip of coffee, his first cup of the morning, and exhaled. "Yeah, you and me both. On the one hand, I wonder if Preston was telling the truth. Because he was shot to death. Maybe the three guys did want him dead. But on the other hand, if he was lying, then who else could have shot him?"

"Well, the man told you that he knew which one of the guys had killed Gavin," pointed out Caleb.

Beanie nodded. "Dennis Woodard."

"Preston told you that Woodard shot him," said Stevie. "And that cab driver told you that Woodard asked about getting a ghost gun."

"And Woodard worked for the St. X Postal Department," said Caleb.

Leaning back in his chair, Beanie put the Styrofoam cup on the table. "I was telling Noelle last night that Preston's story, as crazy as it seems, just might be true. Three guys travel to St. Killian to confront the man who duped them into investing in fake bonds, then ran off with the money. Years later, they find out the guy is still alive, and—"

"Because of Gavin de Grac, right?" asked Stevie. "He hired the private detective to confirm the ex-girlfriend's story."

"de Grac told the other three," said Caleb. "But maybe de Grac didn't think they would want to confront Preston. After all, like you said, years had passed."

"And de Grac didn't seem to care anymore," said Beanie. "But, the other guys might have still been nursing grudges. So, they decided to come to St. Killian."

"They had to have come to confront Preston," said Caleb.

"Maybe they were going to demand that he give them their money back," suggested Stevie. "Or, else, you know? They could have planned to threaten Preston."

"Gavin de Grac might have tried to talk them out of their plan," said Beanie. "He might have anticipated things escalating into violence. So, he decides to warn Preston. Maybe the guys found out that de Grac warned Preston. The four guys could have argued. Then Dennis Woodard shot de Grac."

"Well, at that point, the men probably panicked," said Caleb. "Then started making stupid decisions, the worst of which—other than killing de Grac—was leaving de Grac's body on the beach."

"Then they decided to frame Preston," said Beanie.

"Makes sense," said Stevie. "They probably hoped it would look like what we all assumed—de Grac confronted Preston, and Preston shot de Grac."

"So is Janvier going to arrest Dennis Woodard?" asked Caleb.

Beanie scoffed. "Why? Because I told him that Zach Preston told me that Woodard killed de Grac and then shot him? That's second-hand, secondhand information."

"Fourth-hand information," said Stevie.

"Believe it or not," said Beanie, "Fields told me that Janvier does want to talk to Dennis Woodard. Actually, he plans to talk to all three men. But, until he interviews them, he's sticking to his theory that Preston killed de Grac."

"Who does Janvier think killed Preston?" asked Stevie.

Beanie said, "He didn't share that information with me, not surprisingly."

"You think Woodard shot Preston?" asked Caleb.

"I'm not sure," said Beanie. "Preston didn't get the chance to tell me how he found out that Woodard was the man who killed de Grac. And if Woodard shot Preston, then how did Woodard find out that Preston knew Woodard was the real killer?"

Stevie shook his head. "Maybe you need to have another talk with Dennis Woodard."

Beanie nodded. "I think you're right."

39

"What did the letter say?" asked Beanie, taking a sip of coffee.

Sitting at the kitchen table across from him, Noelle picked up her mug and stared into it.

At seven a.m. on a Saturday morning, the house was quiet. A hushed solemnness permeated the air. Beanie's heart was still beating wildly from his wife's grave announcement after she'd walked into the kitchen. Wrapped in her robe, she'd shuffled to the coffee maker and said, "I have something to tell you."

Panic and worry had gripped Beanie. He'd been enjoying the solitude. The calm before the storm—said storm being his boys, Ethan, and Evan, who were still asleep. In an hour or so, they'd be up, as rambunctious and recalcitrant as ever, demanding his attention.

Staring at his wife, he'd tortured himself with dozens of scenarios.

What could she want to tell him? Something good? Something bad? Something life-changing? Something he wouldn't believe? Or know how to process?

Beanie had swallowed his apprehension. "What?"

Noelle made him wait until she'd made her coffee. His wife had been agonizingly slow, taking care with the cream, sugar, and drizzle of honey she liked to add. When she joined him at the table, she took a few sips. With an exaggerated sigh, she'd said, "I opened that letter my dad wrote me."

"Actually," said Noelle, answering his question about the letter's contents, "it was not what I expected."

"So he's not a changed man?" asked Beanie. "He doesn't want to meet the kids?"

"He hasn't changed, so he couldn't tell that lie," said Noelle. "And he didn't mention the boys, so maybe he's given up on meeting them."

"Really?" asked Beanie, doubtful.

"He's got to know by now that I do not want him in my kids' lives," said Noelle, her eyes flashing with indignation. "He needs to stop badgering Mom about seeing his grandkids. All he does is put her in the middle. And then she badgers me, even though she knows what I'm going to say."

"I just think your mom is hoping one day you'll change your mind," said Beanie.

"Well, I won't," said Noelle.

"Why not?" pressed Beanie.

Noelle frowned. "You know why not."

"Okay, yeah, I know your father used to kill people," said Beanie. "But, you know he's not going to hurt the boys."

"My father doesn't have to physically hurt the boys to hurt the boys," said Noelle. "Just the fact that Josue Chartres is their grandfather is bad enough. They're going to have to live with that stigma. With that notoriety. That horrible infamy."

Beanie took another sip of coffee. "Are you worried people will think the boys are going to be like their grandfather? Cold-blooded killers?"

Noelle pierced him with a sharp glare. "That's not funny, Roland. Because you know some people will think that."

Shrugging, Beanie said, "Elle, you can't be the thought police. People will think what they want to think. Ethan and Evan will grow up and prove them wrong."

"I know that, but …" Noelle rubbed her forehead.

"Tell me about the letter," requested Beanie.

Noelle exhaled. "Well, my dad apologized for not being the father I deserved. And then he said he wanted to make it up to me."

"Make it up to you how?" asked Beanie.

Shaking her head, Noelle said, "He wants to give me … money."

Confused, Beanie asked, "Money?"

"He's got a stash," said Noelle. "He swears it's not blood money. It's profits from legitimate investments, he claims."

"How much money?"

"Who cares?" Noelle rolled her eyes. "Doesn't matter. I'm not taking a dime from him."

"Probably for the best," said Beanie. He doubted Josue Chartres had any legitimate finances. Any investments the man had made would most likely have been done with laundered funds.

"However …"

"There's more?"

"Dad says if I refuse the money, which I will, and he knows that then he plans to leave it all to Ethan and Evan," said Noelle.

Beanie gaped at his wife. "What?"

"I don't know what to do," said Noelle. "Mom says I can take the money and give it to charity."

Nodding, Beanie said, "Or you could—"

A series of beeps filled the air.

"That your phone?" asked Noelle, standing.

"Yeah, but it's just a text," said Beanie, removing the phone from the oversized pocket of his robe. "I can check it later."

"Just check it now," said Noelle. "I'm kind of over-talking about my dad. And I need to get the boys up. They've got a birthday party this afternoon, and we need to get a gift before we go."

As his wife left the kitchen, Beanie accessed the text.

The message was from Officer Damon Fields.

Beanie read the text. *Hey, give me a call when you get a minute. Info re Dennis Woodard.*

His curiosity piqued, Beanie dialed Fields' cell number. Since his conversation with Caleb and Stevie two days ago, he'd been trying to contact Woodard. He wanted to question the man regarding the deaths of both Gavin de Grac and Zach Preston. So far, Woodard hadn't returned his calls, texts, or emails.

"What's going on with Dennis Woodard?" asked Beanie when Fields answered. "Did Janvier question him?"

"Well, he was going to," said Fields. "But not anymore."

"Why not?" asked Beanie, wondering if the detective had decided not to believe his statement concerning the events that had taken place at Zach Preston's shotgun house in Seashell Estates.

Fields said, "Because Dennis Woodard is dead … "

40

"So, Dennis Woodard, who may or may not have killed both Gavin de Grac and Zach Preston, is dead?" asked Vivian, frowning as she took a bite of her pastry.

"Right," said Beanie, taking a sip of the latte he'd bought from the Hullabaloo coffee cart in Pourciau Square.

After an early morning conversation with Officer Fields, Beanie dropped into Vivian's office to give her the latest details in the Gavin de Grac/Zach Preston murder investigation. Vivian suggested they get out of the office, where she'd been cooped up for most of the morning, trapped on a conference call with the *Palmchat Gazette*'s legal team. Beanie suggested Pourciau Square, which wouldn't be crowded at ten in the morning. Vivian agreed, and they set out, strolling along the sidewalk on a breezy, sunny day.

Vivian dabbed at the corners of her mouth with a paper napkin. "How?"

"You remember the bad car accident on the west side of the island a few days ago?" asked Beanie, propping an elbow on the wooden bistro table. "Only one car was involved, and it blew up upon impact, killing the driver."

Vivian flipped her long braids over her shoulder. "What does that have to do with Dennis Woodard?"

"That driver was Dennis Woodard," explained Beanie.

"And during your last communication with Zach Preston, he told you that Woodard killed Gavin de Grac."

Nodding, Beanie said, "And he told me that Woodard shot him."

"But you have no idea how Preston found out that Woodard allegedly killed de Grac."

"Initially, I didn't," said Beanie, taking another sip of coffee. "But Fields said the police recovered texts from Preston's phone. Seems that someone was communicating with Preston about de Grac's murder."

Vivian's eyes narrowed. "Someone?"

"The police are still tracing the texts and calls," said Beanie. "But the person who texted Preston claimed that Woodard was the killer. And I'm not surprised that Preston believed that. He knew that the anonymous tip about the murder weapon planted in his backyard was called in from the St. Xavier Postal Department."

"That's where Woodard worked," interjected Vivian.

"And Woodard asked Jared, the cab driver, about acquiring a ghost gun," said Beanie.

Vivian shook her head. "That's not enough evidence to prove that Woodard killed anybody."

Stroking his jaw, Beanie said, "You know, I've been thinking about that night when I found Gavin de Grac dead on Mango Beach."

"Thinking what about it?"

"I was at a 4th of July party my cousin's girlfriend hosted," started Beanie. "At one point, I went to get a beer from the table my cousin and his friends had set up on the beach near the water. While I was walking between the sand dunes, three guys stopped me and asked for directions to Mango Cove."

"So, wait a minute." Vivian frowned at him. "Are you saying that you encountered Archie Hall, Tarragon Ungaro, and Dennis Woodward *before* Gavin de Grac was killed?"

"If Preston was telling the truth and Dennis Woodard killed de Grac, then yes," said Beanie, marveling at the sudden realization. "I talked to the men *before* Woodard killed de Grac."

"Allegedly," amended Vivian. "According to Zach Preston."

"Based on the text messages he was sent," said Beanie.

"So, let's say Woodard did kill de Grac," began Vivian. "What's his motive?"

"Zach Preston scammed all three of the men out of five thousand each," said Beanie. "Preston claimed that Gavin wanted to forgive and forget, but maybe Dennis Woodard couldn't do that."

"Okay, that gives Woodard a motive for killing Preston," said Vivian. "But why would Woodard kill Gavin." Beanie pondered the question. "All I can think is … Preston was right. Gavin warned Preston about the men's plan to go after him. I think Dennis got upset with Gavin, the men argued, got into a gunfight, and then Woodard shot and killed Gavin."

41

Stevie asked, "So … who do you think sent Preston the texts about Woodard killing de Grac?"

Sitting across from Stevie at a table in the *Palmchat Gazette* breakroom, Beanie reflected on the story he'd written two days before: CAR CRASH VICTIM CONNECTED TO RECENT HOMICIDES. In the article, Beanie proposed the theory that Dennis Woodard had traveled to St. Killian to kill Zach Preston. Woodard's motive had been to stop Preston from telling the police that Woodard had murdered Gavin de Grac.

Beanie said, "Had to have been one of the other men Preston stole from. When I think about this whole situation, I believe that the three men—Archie, Dennis, and Tarragon—came to St. Killian to get revenge on Zach Preston. They probably thought Gavin de Grac would help them, but instead, de Grac warned Preston."

"So, Woodard killed de Grac because he warned Preston," said Stevie. "And then the guys panicked."

"They went back to St. X," said Beanie, picking up the narrative.

"And one of them had a crisis of conscience or something?" asked Stevie.

"Must have," said Beanie. "And that person—either Archie or Tarragon—decided to come clean to Preston and sent him texts revealing Woodard as the killer."

"Why not come clean to the police?" asked Stevie.

"Maybe Archie or Tarragon, whoever sent the texts, didn't really want to get Woodard in trouble with the cops," said Beanie. "Remember, these guys were friends."

"Still, I wonder why Woodard didn't get rid of Archie or Tarragon," said Stevie. "He killed de Grac."

"Yeah, but I don't think Woodard meant to kill de Grac," said Beanie.

"You think he meant to scare him?" asked Stevie.

Standing, Beanie shrugged. "I think there was an argument. Then a gun battle. And Gavin ended up dead."

Back at his desk, Beanie sat down to check his emails, but his desk phone buzzed.

"Come to the conference room," demanded Vivian. "Now."

Moments later, Beanie entered the conference room. Vivian was on the other side of the room, at the far end of the table. Sitting on the edge, she stared at the large television that descended from the ceiling via remote control.

"What's up?" asked Beanie as he walked toward his boss.

Vivian faced him.

Her stern scowl was unnerving, but Beanie tried not to jump to the worst conclusions.

"We've been scooped," announced Vivian, lips pursed as she frowned.

"Scooped?" echoed Beanie, glancing at the screen. The reporter, perfectly coiffed with a stern expression, was wrapping up a story about tourists who'd suffered alcohol poisoning during a pub crawl.

"I thought Stevie covered the pub crawl poisoning?" asked Beanie, glancing over his shoulder at his boss.

"I don't mean that story," snapped Vivian. "Check out what's coming up next …"

" … with Detective Philippi Janvier …" said the anchor.

The mention of the detective's name arrested Beanie's attention toward the television screen again.

"The St. Killian detective spoke exclusively to investigative reporter Corliss Hudson concerning the murder of a local St. Killian man whose death has a connection to a horrible car accident …"

Fuming with consternation and a touch of envy, Beanie shook his head. "Since when does Janvier give interviews."

"Since the reporter isn't you," said Vivian.

"Well, it's not like I've never tried to get an exclusive," said Beanie, aware of the slight censure in his boss's tone. "All he ever gives me is no comment."

"And why is that?" asked Vivian, arms crossed as she focused on the screen.

Giving his boss a sideways glance, Beanie wondered if Vivian felt he hadn't done enough to mend fences with Janvier and thus repair the relationship so the newspaper could count on the detective as a trusted source. He worried she thought he should relax his hold on the grudge against Janvier he held so tightly. He worried that maybe his boss was right.

Beanie said nothing as the shot switched to Janvier and Corliss Hudson. Standing a few feet apart, the detective and the investigative reporter appeared to be outside the St. Killian police station. Filmed on a sunny, windy day, Janvier's lavender tie, paired with a beige linen suit, flapped over his shoulder in the gusty breeze. "Detective Janvier, what can you tell our viewers about the deadly car accident which occurred a week prior and its connection to the murder of Gavin de Grac?" asked Corliss.

"The Crime Scene team discovered that the car did not explode because of the accident," said Janvier.

Stunned by the revelation, Beanie removed his phone from his pants pocket and opened his notetaking app.

Janvier went on, "There is strong evidence that the car accident was staged. We now know that the victim, a Mr. Dennis Woodard from St. Xavier, was shot to death and placed in the driver's seat of the car. Then the car was deliberately crashed, and finally, the vehicle was purposely set on fire."

Beanie's thumbs typed furiously.

"As I am sure you know," said Janvier, "certain members of the media have suggested that Dennis Woodard traveled to St. Killian to kill a man named Zachary Preston, who had previously been arrested for the murder of Gavin de Grac. But, that is not possible ..."

"Why not?" asked Corliss.

Janvier gave the camera a smug smile.

Beanie knew the detective's sly look was directed at him. Beanie was sure that Janvier had been referring to him when he mentioned 'certain members of the media.'

Janvier said to Corliss, "The forensic pathologist has determined that Dennis Woodard had been dead for at least five days before his body was recovered from the burning vehicle, which means that Woodward could not have killed Zach Preston ..."

"Dead for five days," whispered Beanie, shocked by the stunning details.

Vivian glanced at him. "Did you know that?"

Shaking his head, Beanie said, "Fields didn't mention it."

"Because Fields didn't know," said Vivian. "Because Janvier probably made sure that Fields didn't have access to that information. Because Janvier didn't want Fields to tell you."

Again, Beanie heard the frustration in Vivian's tone. He was certain her irritation stemmed from her belief that if Janvier was Beanie's source, information would come from the detective assigned to the case. Beanie wouldn't have to rely on Fields's secondhand details.

"However, I am quite certain this malfeasance was perpetrated by an unknown person who sent text messages to Zachary Preston," said Janvier. "The text to Mr. Preston suggested that Mr. Woodard had killed Gavin de Grac."

"Do you have any idea who sent the text messages to Preston?" asked Corliss.

"Not at this time. However, we do have several leads," said Janvier.

"I doubt that," quipped Beanie, but not loud enough for Vivian to hear him.

Janvier said, "I personally believe this unknown person is the real killer of Gavin de Grac, Zachary Preston, and Dennis Woodard."

42

I personally believe this unknown person is the real killer of Gavin de Grac, Zachary Preston, and Dennis Woodard ...

Detective Janvier's somber assessment of a cold-blooded murderer sent a chill through Beanie even though the robust St. Killian sun shone hot and bright at eleven in the morning. Sitting on the upper decks of the ferry, Beanie felt the full brunt of strong rays that sparkled over the slightly choppy waves of the Caribbean.

Since Janvier's jaw-dropping interview with the local news station yesterday evening, Beanie had ruminated about the shocking details all night. After discussing the bombshell revelations with Vivian and Stevie, Beanie shared more of his thoughts with Noelle while they tidied up the kitchen following dinner.

This morning when he'd arrived at the *Palmchat Gazette* office, he'd been headed to the break room for his first cup of coffee of the morning when Vivian waylaid him in the hallway. "Come to my office," she demanded, leading the way.

As Beanie settled into one of the chairs in front of her desk, Vivian said, "I was thinking all night about the unknown person who texted Zach Preston."

"Yeah, I didn't get much sleep," admitted Beanie. "I kept thinking, if Janvier is right, then one of those old men—either Archie or Tarragon—is a killer. But which one? How can I find out?"

"I have an idea," said Vivian, a hint of a smug smile playing at her lips.

Curious, Beanie said, "I'm listening."

"Leo reminded me of a story I worked on in South Sudan involving —what else—government corruption. I'd heard a rumor that a defense minister was leaking military strategy to a faction of rebels. The insurgents funded their campaign with conflict diamonds and promised to pay the defense minister in blood stones. Despite his position, this man was addicted to gambling and owed money to the Russian mafia."

"Sounds dangerous," said Beanie.

Vivian said, "I needed to find out which defense minister was sharing secrets."

"And did you?" asked Beanie.

"I employed a simple but effective tactic," said Vivian. "I played them off each other."

"That worked?" asked Beanie.

Nodding, Vivian said, "One of the men—I'll call him Minister A— denied leaking military strategy. The other man—Minister B—said Minister A was lying and that actually Minister A was the culprit."

Beanie rubbed his jaw. "And you were able to figure out which man was lying?"

Vivian said, "People who are falsely accused will deny the accusation. But liars will tell you another lie."

"So, Minister B was leaking the strategies."

"I was able to prove that he was," said Vivian. "And that's what I want you to do. You need to figure out which one of those old coots is the killer. Archie or Tarragon."

Frowning, Beanie said, "And you want me to play them off each other."

"Right."

"You want me to lie to them," said Beanie, unsure of the strategy.

"Tell Archie that Tarragon pointed the finger at him. And tell Tarragon that Archie said he's the killer."

Vivian nodded. "Right."

"I don't know …" Beanie hedged.

"What don't you know?"

"What if it doesn't work?"

"Well, you won't know if it works or not," said Vivian, "unless you try to make it work."

43

"Tarragon lied to you," said Archie Hall. "I didn't kill anyone!"

"And why is that?" asked Beanie, sitting across from Hall in the man's dining room. The small space, though clean and sparsely furnished, felt claustrophobic. The atmosphere was dank and humid.

Fifteen minutes ago, as Beanie walked up the driveway toward Archie Hall's house, a stark sense of unease had assailed him. With each step, he'd lost confidence in Vivian's idea to play the old men against each other. Not that he didn't believe in his boss's plan, because he did.

He just wasn't sure it would work in this particular situation.

Archie Hall and Tarragon Ungaro were two old West Indian retirees, not African dignitaries. And he was a young guy they had no reason to fear or respect. On the other hand, Vivian was a good-looking woman whose beauty might have helped her succeed in her quest for the truth.

Staring at Archie Hall, Beanie realized the confidence he lacked was in himself. Vivian's plan relied on cunning trickery. Beanie had never relied on sly stealth when questioning people. He wasn't sure he could fool either of the men into incriminating themselves. He had a feeling this trip to St. X would be a waste of time, as his last trip had been.

Still, when Archie Hall invited him inside the small home, Beanie wasted no time putting Vivian's plan in motion, telling Archie that Tarragon Ungaro had fingered Archie as the person who'd killed Gavin de Grac, Dennis Woodard, and Zach Preston.

Archie let out a deep, mournful exhale. "Tarragon is a dangerous killer."

"You're saying that Tarragon killed Gavin?" asked Beanie.

"And he killed Dennis Woodard and Zach Preston, too."

"How do you know that?"

"Because Tarragon told me he killed them."

"Why would he confess to you?"

Shaking his head, Archie said, "Wasn't a confession. It was a threat."

"A threat?"

"A warning," said Archie. "Tarragon told me to keep my mouth shut about what he'd done to Gavin. And when I told him that I didn't know if I could stay quiet, then Tarragon told me that he'd killed Dennis and Zach Preston. And if I didn't want to be next, then I needed to keep my mouth shut."

"Mr. Hall, Tarragon told me that you killed Gavin, Dennis, and Zach Preston," said Beanie, maintaining the lie as he tried to remember how Vivian had determined which of the African defense ministers was the crook selling military secrets. Was the real culprit the man who'd denied the claims? Or the man who'd tried to deflect the blame? So far, Archie Hall had done both. He'd denied killing Gavin, Dennis, and Zach Preston. And he'd pointed the finger at Tarragon.

"I told you that Tarragon lied—"

"But what if Tarragon goes to the police and tells them you're a cold-blooded killer?" asked Beanie. "What if he tries to frame you?"

"I can't believe that Tarragon would pin these murders on me," said Archie. "We been friends too long. Me and Tarragon belonged to a cricket club. That's how we met. Gavin and Dennis was in the club, too. That's how we all got to know each other. Became friends. The club wasn't anything serious. We weren't very competitive. Just a bunch of guys who liked to get together on Sundays after church. We had some good times. And some bad times ..."

"Bad times?"

A grim scowl crossed Archie Hall's face. "When Zach Preston joined the club. He was a friend of Gavin's. Don't know where they met. But Gavin started telling me, Tarragon, and Dennis that Preston was in investments. Gavin said we could make a lot of money if we invested with Preston."

"So the four of you invested with Preston?" asked Beanie, recalling what Zach Preston had told him.

"Worst mistake we ever made," said Archie. "Preston ran off with our money. We had no choice but to take the loss. Seemed like there was nothing we could do. Police couldn't help. Preston was long gone. Nobody knew where he'd hightailed it off to …"

Cotswold, England, thought Beanie, though he decided to keep that information to himself.

"About a month ago, Gavin contacted me, Dennis, and Tarragon," started Archie. "Said he had something to tell us. Something we wouldn't believe."

"Gavin told you that Zach Preston was still alive?"

Archie nodded. "And Gavin was right. We didn't believe it. But then he showed us some pictures. And it was Preston. Gavin said the photos were recent. He'd hired a private investigator to find out if Zach Preston was still alive."

Remembering the manila folder he'd found in room 729 at the Swaying Palms Inn, Beanie rubbed his jaw.

"And come to find out, Preston wasn't dead, even though Gavin had told us he was," said Archie, shaking his head. "Gavin said it was in some newspaper. Said Preston had died in a car accident over in England."

"So when you, Dennis, and Tarragon found out that Preston was alive, what did you do?"

"We immediately wanted to get our money back," said Archie. "We wanted to contact the police. Tell them that Preston was alive. Then the cops could arrest him, and we could sue him for financial fraud and theft. Me, Dennis, and Tarragon went to St. Killian. Gavin got a motel room for us. Low-rent place in Little Turkey."

"But you didn't file a complaint against Preston," said Beanie.

"Because we couldn't," said Archie. "Gavin had told us that we'd waited too late. The statute of limitations had run out. Gavin said it didn't matter that we had thought Preston was dead all these years and had just found out he was alive. That didn't sit well with none of us."

"You must have been upset."

Archie scoffed, leaning back in his chair. "Me and Dennis was disappointed, but what could we do? We figured that we'd lived all these years without the money, so we'd just live the rest of our lives without it. But Tarragon didn't feel that way …"

Beanie stared at Archie. "How did Tarragon feel?"

"Tarragon was more upset than the rest of us," said Archie. "When Preston took off with his money, it caused problems in his marriage, and his old lady left him. She took their son with her, and he hasn't seen the boy in ten years. He got depressed about that and ended up losing his job. Couldn't find work for a few years. Started drinking. Tarragon just didn't think it was right that Preston was gonna get away with stealing from us. Me and Dennis didn't like it, either, but …"

"But …?" prompted Beanie.

His expression weary and apprehensive, Archie said, "Tarragon started saying that we should force Preston to return the money he stole from us. Said Preston needed to pay."

"And did you and Dennis agree?"

Archie sighed. "Me and Dennis didn't think that was a good idea. Dennis was telling Tarragon to just let it go. Forget about it. Let bygones be bygones. Tarragon said he couldn't do that. I tried to calm Tarragon down. I thought I had. But, turned out, the next day, Tarragon convinced Dennis to help him get a gun."

"So, Tarragon told Dennis to ask the cab driver about a ghost gun?"

Suspicion flickered across Archie's face. "How you know about that?"

"I talked to the cab driver," said Beanie. "He said he refused to help Dennis get a gun."

"Tarragon ended up buying a gun from some guy in Handweg," said

Archie. "Some old friend."

"Do you know the old friend's name?" asked Beanie, thinking about the address on the back of the grocery receipt found in the file that contained photos of Zach Preston.

"I don't," said Archie. "Dennis went with Tarragon to get the gun. Then they returned to the motel. Tarragon started talking about confronting Preston. Dennis and I tried to talk him out of it. We wanted to head back to St. X, but Tarragon said Preston shouldn't get away with what he'd done. So, Dennis and I didn't try to stop him when he said he was leaving to confront Preston."

"And did Tarragon leave the motel?"

"He did," said Archie. "Tarragon called a cab and then went outside the motel room to wait for it to come."

"And did you and Dennis go outside, too, to wait for the cab?"

Archie shook his head. "We didn't leave the motel."

A jolt passed through Beanie. "You and Dennis stayed at the motel? You didn't go with Tarragon to confront Preston?"

"We stayed at the motel," said Archie.

"So … you and Dennis didn't go to Mango Beach with Tarragon?"

"I told you we didn't," said Archie, glaring at Beanie. "Me and Dennis stayed at the motel. Tarragon went on to Mango Beach by himself."

Beanie nodded, glancing away. Archie Hall was lying. Beanie distinctly recalled encountering Tarragon, Dennis, and Archie on Mango Beach the night Gavin had been murdered. He remembered Tarragon mentioning Dennis by his name. Archie Hall had been cranky and cursing. He'd walked away, refusing directions as he'd disappeared into the tall beach grass.

"We didn't want to confront Preston," Archie continued. "Tell you the truth, I was thinking the whole trip was a bad idea. I just wanted to get home. So, a few hours later, Dennis and I went to get something to eat for dinner. When we got back to the motel, Tarragon was there. He was sweating and pacing, and crying. And he had blood all over his shirt."

Recalling Zach Preston's description of the bloody shirt, Beanie asked. "You're talking about the shirt with the Aerie Islands national cricket team logo on it?"

Nodding, Archie said, "That's the one. Tarragon never set foot in the Aerie Islands, but he followed their cricket team."

"How did Tarragon explain the blood on his T-shirt ?" asked Beanie

"Tarragon told me and Dennis that he had shot Gavin," said Archie, his face lined with remorse. "Dennis and I couldn't believe it. I still can't. And when I think about it now, I know we should have called the police."

"But you didn't."

"I know Tarragon didn't mean to kill him," said Archie. "But, he was so filled with rage and hate over Preston, he wasn't thinking straight."

"And then what did you do?"

"Dennis and I packed Tarragon's bag, and we got our bags, and we just left. We walked to a jitney stop and then went to catch a late-night ferry back to St. X."

"What happened when you returned to St. X?"

"We decided not to say anything," Archie said. "We decided to pretend none of it had happened. When you came looking for me, and my wife told me you had questions about Gavin and Preston, I didn't call you back because I couldn't. I had promised to keep my mouth shut. But I was worried that Tarragon was gonna get connected to Gavin's murder. But then Tarragon said he could fix things."

"Fix things how?"

"Said he had a plan to make it look like Preston had killed Gavin," said Archie. "Me and Dennis thought Tarragon was crazy, but he claimed it would work. He said Preston would finally go to jail where he belonged."

"So Tarragon framed Preston for Gavin's murder?"

Archie nodded. "Tarragon had kept that bloody T-shirt with Gavin's blood on it. He buried that T-shirt and the gun he'd used to kill Gavin in Preston's backyard."

Beanie scratched his jaw. "So, you're saying Tarragon buried the T-shirt he'd been wearing when he killed Gavin?"

Archie Hall glared at him. "That was the T-shirt with Gavin's blood on it. What other T-shirt could he have buried?"

"Yeah, but …"

"Listen, I know what Tarragon did was wrong," said Archie, his gaze intense. "And maybe you think he needs to spend the rest of his life in prison, but he didn't mean to do none of this. He went crazy because of his hatred of Zach Preston."

"Mr. Hall, you have to go to the police," began Beanie.

"I can't do that," insisted Archie. "Tarragon was serious when he said he would kill me. And I don't think you should put none of what I told you in the paper, or Tarragon will kill you, too. I probably shouldn't have even told you."

"Why did you?" asked Beanie.

Shaking his head, Archie Hall said, "When you told me Tarragon was lying on me, I had to tell you the truth but not so you can put it in the paper. Just so you can know the truth. And sometimes, that's enough."

"And sometimes, just knowing the truth is not enough, Mr. Hall," advised Beanie. "Sometimes, you have to tell the truth. If Tarragon is a killer— "

"He is," insisted Archie.

Beanie said, "Then you need to give a statement to the police."

"What if they don't believe me? I don't have any proof," said Archie Hall. "My word ain't going to be good enough."

"Mr. Hall—"

"I think you should leave now," said Archie Hall, rising to his feet.

"Look, I know you might be afraid of Tarragon," said Beanie, remaining seated despite the hostility in the man's gaze. "But—"

"I would like you to leave, please," said Archie.

Frustrated by the old man's misguided stubbornness, Beanie stood. "Mr. Hall, if you change your mind about talking to the police—"

"I won't," said Archie Hall, walking toward the front door.

Saying nothing, Beanie followed.

Moments later, he stood on the porch, staring at the door that Archie Hall had slammed in his face.

44

After concluding his conversation with Archie Hall, Beanie called a cab to take him to Tarragon Ungaro's house.

In the back seat of the car, he tried to gather his thoughts. Tried to come to some sort of conclusion about Archie Hall. Was the man a victim? Or the villain?

Beanie wasn't sure.

He knew Archie Hall had lied about not being on Mango Beach the night Gavin died. And he was fairly certain that Tarragon Ungaro hadn't buried his cricket T-shirt in Zach Preston's backyard. Another lie. But why had Archie Hall lied?

Beanie figured it depended on whether or not Archie Hall had been telling the truth about Tarragon killing Zach Preston. If Tarragon was innocent, then Archie might have been trying to deflect the blame from himself. Like the corrupt African defense minister, Archie could have been trying to frame another person for his crimes.

But, if Tarragon was guilty, then maybe Archie Hall had lied because he didn't want anyone to know he'd been near the crime scene. Beanie could envision a scenario where the three men had confronted Gavin on the beach. Archie might have witnessed the argument between

Gavin and Tarragon Ungaro. Hall might have watched in helpless horror as Tarragon shot Gavin.

Maybe, Beanie conceded to himself as he walked up the steps to Tarragon's porch after the cab dropped him off in front of Tarragon Ungaro's home.

Why Archie Hall would lie about Tarragon burying the Aerie Islands T-shirt in Preston's backyard didn't make sense. Tarragon was almost four times bigger than Zach Preston. If the police had uncovered Tarragon's T-shirt, they would have immediately known that it couldn't have belonged to Preston. The T-shirt would have been too large for Preston, who was slight and gaunt. The T-shirt the St. Killian cops had found must have appeared to have been Preston's size. So, if the T-shirt didn't belong to Preston or Tarragon, then whose T-shirt had the cops found?

Standing at Tarragon's front door, Beanie took a deep breath and knocked on the cracked, peeling wood.

When it opened moments later, Tarragon Ungaro scowled at him.

"I don't have no comment," grunted the old man, his voice gruff and raspy.

"Mr. Ungaro—"

"You're from the newspaper," said Tarragon. "I remember you. I didn't have nothing to say when you came here before, and I don't have nothing to say now, so—"

"Mr. Ungaro, I have some questions about the murders of Gavin de Grac, Dennis Woodard, and Zach Preston," said Beanie.

Tarragon's green eyes were wary. "Why are you asking me about those murders?"

"Could we go inside and talk?" asked Beanie. "Please …"

Following a long, baleful stare and a weary exhale, Tarragon Ungaro turned, leaving the door open so Beanie could enter the small, shotgun house.

"Come on into the kitchen." Tarragon waddled through the living area, his massive girth shifting from side to side as he took one laborious step after the other. Beanie glanced at the man's spindly legs, bound in diabetic socks, and wondered how they supported his gelatinous mass.

"Now, why are you asking me about those murders?" asked Tarragon, grunting as he dropped into a chair at a round table.

"Did you kill those men, Mr. Ungaro?" asked Beanie. "Did you shoot Gavin, Dennis, and Zach Preston?" "I don't know what you're talking about," said Tarragon, shaking his head. "I didn't shoot nobody. I am not a killer."

"Mr. Ungaro, Archie Hall says that you are a cold-blooded murderer," said Beanie. "I spoke with him before I came here. I'm going to be honest with you. I wasn't honest with him. I lied to him. I told him that you'd told me that he killed Gavin, Dennis, and Zach—"

"Why would you do that?" demanded Tarragon.

"I wanted to see what he would say," said Beanie. "I wanted to see if he would deny your claims."

A flicker of worry clouded Tarragon's face. "And did he?"

"No, he didn't," said Beanie. "He immediately pointed the finger at you. He said you were pointing the finger at him to save yourself. But I don't think that's not true. I think Archie Hall murdered those men. You can't let him get away with that."

Folding his arms across his massive midsection, Tarragon shook his head. "I don't believe you. Arch wouldn't say nothing like that. He wouldn't try to blame no murders on me."

"Archie Hall told me that you killed Gavin de Grac," said Beanie, sitting across from the man. "Mr. Hall also said you killed Dennis Woodard and Zach Preston."

"I don't believe you …" Tarragon shook his head. "Arch wouldn't say that."

"He did say that," insisted Beanie. "He accused you of being a cold-blooded murderer. But you and I both know that he's the real killer."

Exhaling, Tarragon dragged a hand down his damp face. "Arch never meant to kill nobody. What happened to Gavin wasn't supposed to happen. It was an accident. Wasn't nobody supposed to end up dead. That wasn't the plan."

"What about Dennis Woodard?" asked Beanie. "Was his death an accident, too?"

Tarragon said, "Dennis died in a car crash. The car exploded."

Despite the man's baleful glare, Beanie continued. "The police have determined that Woodard was already dead when the car crashed and burned. Woodard had actually been dead for about five days. The car accident was staged."

"I don't know nothing about that," snapped Tarragon.

"I know you don't," said Beanie. "But I think Archie Hall killed Dennis and staged that accident."

Tarragon shook his head. "Arch wouldn't have killed Dennis. They was good friends. And Arch wouldn't blame no murders on me."

Shaking his head, Beanie said, "One of the pieces of evidence that tied Zach Preston to the murder of Gavin de Grac was a bloody T-shirt. But not just any T-shirt. A bloody Aerie Islands Starfish T-shirt. Like the one you're wearing, which Archie said you buried in Preston's backyard."

Frowning, Tarragon looked down at the threadbare T-shirt, then back at Beanie. "Wasn't my Starfish shirt with Gavin's blood on it."

"I know that," said Beanie. "It was Archie Hall's Starfish T-shirt with Gavin's blood on it, right?"

Tarragon exhaled. "Archie was supposed to get rid of that T-shirt. When he got back to the motel the night Gavin was killed, me and Dennis saw the blood all on his shirt."

"How did he explain that?"

"Arch said Gavin shot at him," said Tarragon. "He said Gavin turned on him."

"Why would Gavin turn on Archie?"

"Arch said Gavin wanted to protect Preston from us," said Tarragon, shaking his head. "It didn't make sense to me and Dennis, but Arch said Gavin pulled a gun on him to stop Arch from confronting Preston. So, then Arch and Gavin tussled. Gavin shot at Arch. And then Arch shot and killed Gavin with the gun he got from Dennis's friend. Arch told us he was going to burn that T-shirt, but he must have planned to use it to frame Preston."

"I'm sure that's what he did," said Beanie.

Tarragon said, "I know that's what Arch did. He told me and Dennis he framed Preston. Said he did it because he wanted to make sure Preston ended up in jail where he belonged. Dennis didn't like that. Told Arch it was wrong. I thought it was wrong, too, but I had gave my word that I wasn't going to say anything, and so I didn't. But what Arch did weigh on me. I couldn't sleep. I kept thinking the cops was gonna find out what Arch had did."

"Mr. Ungaro, listen, I know Archie is your friend, but—"

The doorbell rang.

Beanie started at the jarring chimes. "You expecting someone?"

Struggling to his feet, Tarragon said, "My neighbor sometimes brings me a plate of food. She thinks I eat too much fish and not enough goat. Let me get rid of her."

As the large man lumbered to the door, Beanie's phone rang.

He checked the Caller-ID. Fields, Damon.

"Hey, what's going on?" asked Beanie.

"Where are you?" asked Fields. "I called the *Palmchat Gazette*, but you didn't answer. I wanted to meet for lunch. Got new information about the de Grac, Preston, and Woodard cases."

"I'm in St. X," said Beanie. "I doubt I'll be back in time for lunch."

"Interesting that you're in St. Xavier," said Fields.

"Why is that?"

"Janvier is planning to call the St. X police department and have them bring in Archie Hall," said Fields. "He wants to question Hall for the murders of de Grac, Preston, and Woodard."

"What? Why?"

"Turns out, Dennis Woodard's body was recovered from a rental car," said Fields. "The credit card used to rent the car belonged to Archie Hall's wife, Lottie Hall. Also, according to ferry records, Archie Hall bought two tickets to St. Killian several days before Preston was killed.

Finally, the texts Preston received were sent from a phone that belongs to Lottie Hall."

"When does Janvier plan to question Archie Hall?" asked Beanie.

"He's hoping to head to St. X tonight," said Fields.

"Can you let him know that he needs to interview Tarragon Ungaro," said Beanie.

"Why does he need to talk to Tarragon Ungaro?"

"Janvier is right about Archie Hall," said Beanie. "I'm actually at Tarragon Ungaro's house right now. He can give Janvier details about—"

"Archie, no, don't!" Tarragon yelled, his raspy voice laced with terror and confusion. "What are you doing? Stop!"

His head whipping toward the living room, Beanie jumped up, dropping his phone as Archie Hall hit Tarragon across the head with a large, black gun.

45

"Mr. Ungaro! Oh my God!"

Propelled into action by the blood trailing from the deep gash above the man's right eye, Beanie ran to the couch and dropped to one knee next to the man.

"Get away from him!" commanded Archie Hall.

"We need to call 911," said Beanie, hands trembling as he tried to access Tarragon's wound. "He's bleeding bad. We need to get him to a hospital!"

"I said get away from him," said Archie Hall. "On your feet. Now. And move over there by the television."

After complying with the man's orders, Beanie asked, "Are you just going to let him bleed to death?"

Archie Hall shrugged. "Might be for the best."

"What? To let Tarragon die? Guess I'm not surprised," said Beanie. "You killed Gavin de Grac."

"Not on purpose," said Archie. "Gavin wasn't supposed to die."

"What about Dennis Woodard? And Zach Preston? Were they supposed to die, or not?" asked Beanie, trying to glance around the living room without attracting the older man's attention. He needed a weapon. Something he could throw at Archie. Something to distract the man so he could get away.

Across from the couch, a television sat on a wooden console. An old careworn leather lounger was shoved into the corner to the left of the front door. On the coffee table, small jars made of ceramic and porcelain were randomly placed around magazines arranged in the design of a fan.

His heart sinking at the dearth of options, Beanie tried to ignore the fear and disappointment.

"Preston deserved to die," said Archie.

"And Dennis?"

Archie shook his head. "Shouldn't have happened."

"And yet it did," said Beanie.

"But it wouldn't have if Dennis hadn't …"

"Hadn't what?" prompted Beanie. "How about this? Why don't you explain everything from the beginning? And how about telling me the truth this time."

Scoffing, Archie Hall said, "Everything I told you was the truth up until the part where Gavin told us that we couldn't file charges against Preston because the statute of limitations had run out."

Trying to remember what Archie Hall had told him, Beanie said, "You claimed that Tarragon was livid, but you and Dennis were resolved to let things go."

Chuckling, Archie said, "I was livid. Tarragon and Dennis were okay with letting Preston get away with what he'd done. But I couldn't do that."

"But there was nothing you could do," said Beanie.

"Actually, there was something I could do," said Archie. "I knew how I could make Preston pay for what he'd done. But I would need a gun."

"So you could kill Zach Preston?"

Shaking his head, Archie said, "So I could get our money back. That's all I wanted to do. Get what Preston owed us. That's what I told Dennis. The two of us talked one night while Tarragon was sleeping. Dennis told me he would ask the cab driver about getting a gun."

Recalling his conversation with Jared, the cab driver, which he figured it would be best not to reveal to Archie Hall, Beanie asked, "And what happened?"

"Cab driver couldn't help him," said Archie. "So Dennis said he would ask a friend who lived in Handweg, and the friend got Dennis the gun."

"And Dennis gave that gun to you," said Beanie.

Archie said, "As I said, I explained to Dennis that I was not planning to hurt Preston. I only wanted to use the gun to force the man to give us our money back."

"What if Preston didn't have the money?"

"A crook like Preston would have money stashed somewhere," said Archie. "And as I explained to Dennis, I did not want all of Preston's money. Just our fair share. Only what Preston had stolen from us."

"And Dennis was okay with that?"

"Said he was," said Archie. "The next day, however, Tarragon found the gun and confronted me and Dennis about it. So I came clean. Tarragon didn't like the idea of me trying to force Preston to return our money. We argued about it. I wanted to confront Preston. Tarragon didn't want me to do it."

"But you did anyway?"

"I finally got tired of arguing with Tarragon," said Archie. "I told him and Dennis that I didn't need them to come with me to confront Preston. But, in the end, Dennis and Tarragon decided to go with me because they were not going to let me confront Preston alone. So I called a cab and went outside the motel room to wait for it. Tarragon joined me outside."

"You took a cab to Preston's house?"

"The beach shack in Mango Cove," said Archie. "Not his place in Seashell Estates. We had tried to go there before to confront Preston, but Dennis and Tarragon got cold feet, so we went back to the motel."

"How'd you know about Preston's place on the beach?"

"From the information the private investigator had given Gavin," said Archie. "There was a whole file on Preston, including his two addresses."

"So the three of you go to Mango Cove …"

"Actually, we got dropped off at Mango Beach," said Archie. "I didn't want to show up on Preston's front door. Give the man time to peek out the window, see us, and then escape out the back of the house. I figured we would do a sneak attack. Surprise Preston. Show up in his backyard. Anyway, the cab driver told us we could cut through the dunes on Mango Beach and get to Mango Cove."

"And that's where the three of you ran into me," said Beanie. "That's how I knew you'd lied to me. When you claimed that you hadn't been walking along Mango Beach the night Gavin died. I remembered you, Dennis, and Tarragon."

Shrugging, Archie said, "Had a feeling that's when you got suspicious of me."

Beanie glanced at Tarragon again. The big man remained out like a light. But Beanie perceived Tarragon's chest rising and falling. But the longer he remained unconscious, the more perilous his situation would become. Beanie had to do something, make some sort of move to get the gun away from Archie—soon.

"So, we got to Preston's shack, but Preston wasn't there," continued Archie. "Dennis and Tarragon wanted to leave. I wanted to stay. Wait and see if Preston showed up. Dennis and Tarragon decided to leave, and so they left. About fifteen minutes later, someone did show up, but it wasn't Preston. It was Gavin de Grac."

"Was Gavin supposed to meet you at Preston's shack?" asked Beanie.

Archie shook his head. "As it turned out, Dennis had secretly called Gavin back when we were at the motel and told him to meet us at Preston's shack. Dennis was worried I was going to do something stupid, according to Gavin."

"I'm guessing Gavin tried to talk you out of confronting Preston?"

"Gavin showed up to tell me I was wasting my time waiting for Preston," said Archie. "Preston wasn't going to show up because Gavin had warned Preston. Gavin told Preston not to come because we were going to confront him."

"And then what happened?"

"Gavin and I argued," said Archie. "And then I headed away from Preston's shack, going the way I'm come, through the sand dunes on the beach. Gavin followed me. He was trying to tell me that I needed to forget about making Preston pay. Said I didn't need to have hate in my heart toward Preston. All the while, I'm thinking, Gavin was supposed to be my friend, and he betrayed me. So, I turned to him, pulled out the gun, and demanded that he call Preston and tell him to come to the Mango Cove beach shack."

"What did Gavin do?"

"Gavin pulled a gun on me," said Archie, a hint of wonderment in his tone. "Didn't even know he had a weapon. So, I shot him. And then he fired a shot at me, but it missed. I shot a second time, and Gavin dropped to the ground."

"You killed him," said Beanie.

"It was an accident," said Archie. "When I saw he had the gun, I thought he was going to shoot me, so I shot first. I did not mean to kill him. I was very broken up when I went to check on him, and he was dead."

"So broken up that you hid his body in the sand dunes?" asked Beanie, not bothering to temper his sarcasm. "So broken up that you framed an innocent man for his murder?"

"Preston was not an innocent man," insisted Archie. "Gavin is dead because of what Preston did. Far as I'm concerned, Gavin's blood is on his hands."

"And Gavin's blood was on your T-shirt," said Beanie. "The T-shirt you buried, along with the gun you used to shoot Gavin, in Preston's backyard."

"I don't regret framing Preston," said Archie. "He got what he deserved, which was to be arrested. Because he was a criminal. And he would have gone to jail, but ..."

"But?"

"Dennis was upset that I framed Preston," said Archie. "After Preston was arrested, Dennis confronted me. Told me I'd gone too far. Told me I wouldn't get away with what I'd done. I took that to mean that he was planning to snitch on me to the cops. Tell the police I'd killed Gavin and framed Preston."

"So you killed Dennis?"

"Didn't want to," said Archie Hall, frowning.

"How did it happen?"

Archie sighed. "I told Dennis I wanted to come clean to the St. Killian cops about my involvement in Gavin's murder. Said I couldn't sleep and felt guilty."

"You lied to Dennis."

Archie glared at him and then said, "I asked Dennis to go with me to St. Killian, and Dennis agreed."

"For moral support?" quipped Beanie. Archie's snarling glare tempered his sarcasm. It wouldn't do any good to anger the man and give him a reason to pull the trigger.

"I told him I wanted to come clean to the St. Killian police about my involvement in Gavin's murder. Dennis agreed to come with me."

"Dennis and I took a ferry to St. Killian," said Archie. "I rented a room at a place that was worse than that Little Turkey dump. Motel in Handweg. Ten dollars a night. Fifteen if you wanted maid service. Then I killed Dennis."

Beanie flinched.

Archie said, "Shot him in the head. The motel room had a small closet. I put him in there. Then I rented a car. I put Dennis' body in the trunk of the rental car, then drove to a remote part of the island. I crashed the car, put Dennis in the front seat, then set the car on fire."

"And you watched him burn," said Beanie, unable to hide his disgust.

"I watched his body burn," said Archie. "He was already dead. He didn't feel the flames."

Sickened by the man's irreverent tone, Beanie said, "And you didn't wonder what people would think when Dennis just disappeared? You didn't think that the police would eventually find out that you were probably the last person to see him alive? You know there's CCTV on the ferries, right? And there would be a record of the car you rented."

Sighing, Archie said, "Guess maybe I didn't think it through. I was hoping Dennis' body would be burned beyond recognition and the cops would think it was an accident ..."

"Well, the St. Killian cops were able to identify Dennis Woodard," said Beanie. "And they don't believe that Woodard traveled to St. Killian to kill Preston, which is what you intended."

Archie shook his head. "That's not what I intended. I never tried to blame Preston's murder on Dennis."

"But Preston received text messages saying that Dennis had killed Gavin," said Beanie. "I'm assuming you sent those."

"I did," confirmed Archie. "But only because I wanted to trick Preston into meeting with me. A few days after Dennis died, I sent Preston a text saying that Dennis Woodard had killed Gavin."

"Why did you blame Dennis?" asked Beanie, glancing at Tarragon. The man was still unconscious. His wound still bled profusely. Panic and anger coursed through Beanie. He needed to do something—maybe anything—to get the gun away from Archie Hall.

Archie shrugged. "Because he was dead."

Disturbed by the man's logic, Beanie said, "And then what?"

"Then I texted Preston that I wanted to meet with him to give him proof of Dennis' crimes," said Archie. "I had no proof, but Preston thought I did, and he agreed to meet me. So, I showed up at Preston's place, and I shot him."

Confused, Beanie tried to remember the night he'd gone to Zach Preston's place and found the man dying from a gunshot wound. Preston had told him that Dennis Woodard had shot him. Beanie was sure of that, and yet—

No, that wasn't right, Beanie realized.

"Mr. Preston, what happened?"

"Shot ... me ... "

"Who shot you? Was it Dennis Woodard?"

"Didn't think he would ... get me ...but ... that rascal ... tried to explain ... "

Despair coursed through Beanie as he shook his head. Preston *hadn't* named Dennis Woodard as his killer. Beanie had assumed Woodard had shot Preston, but only because Preston had told him that Woodard had shot Gavin.

"Who is this?"

"Zach Preston."

"Mr. Preston, I don't think—"

"I know who killed Gavin de Grac."

"Okay, have you called the police?"

"It was Dennis Woodard."

The rascal Preston had been referring to wasn't Dennis Woodard. It was the evil old man pointing a gun at him—Archie Hall.

"So how were you going to stop the police from figuring out that you'd killed Preston?" asked Beanie.

"I didn't really think about trying to cover up the crime," said Archie. "I just wanted him dead. I showed up at his house, then snuck around to the backyard and broke into Preston's house through the patio door. He'd been sitting at the dining room table. When he jumped up and turned, I shot him. Didn't give him a chance to beg for his worthless life."

"And what about my life?" asked Beanie.

Archie Hall frowned.

"Will I have a chance to beg for my life?" asked Beanie, trying to get the words past the lump in his throat. "Or, is my life worthless, too? Are you just going to put a bullet in me, as well?"

Archie frowned. "It's not something I want to do."

"But you have no choice?"

"Despite what you think, I am not a cold-blooded killer."

"You could have fooled me," said Beanie.

"I am a man who was trying to make things right," said Archie with righteous indignation. "Me, Gavin, Dennis, and Tarragon was wronged. Preston had to pay, and I'm not sorry I killed him. He got what he deserved."

"Did Gavin and Dennis get what they deserved?" asked Beanie.

"Those men were your friends. And you killed them. Why? Because your misguided, ill-thought-out revenge plan fell apart?"

"It wasn't misguided," insisted Archie. "It was what Preston deserved, and nobody but him had to die, and nobody but him would have died if Gavin hadn't—"

"Archie, stop … don't do this!" Tarragon moaned, eyes fluttering open as he tried to push himself to a sitting position.

Pointing the gun at Tarragon, Archie said, "Shut up! Don't—"

Beanie grabbed one of the porcelain jars from the coffee table and hurled it at Archie. The object hit the old man against his left ear. Cursing, Archie spun back toward Beanie and fired the pistol. Beanie dove to the floor and belly crawled across the musty rug toward the door, hoping he could get there in time, praying that—

The front door burst open.

"Freeze! Now!" The command ricocheted throughout the living room. "Get down on your knees! Don't move!"

Shaking with relief, Beanie went limp as what seemed like a dozen police officers swarmed into the house, guns aimed as they surrounded Archie Hall.

"The Gavin de Grac murder has to be one of the strangest cases," remarked Noelle, looking fetching in a mint green sundress as she took a sip of her Bellini.

Beanie nodded, as did Officer Damon Fields, sitting next to Amber, who was pretty in pink.

After church, Noelle had invited Damon and Amber to join them at Dizzy Jenny's for a late afternoon lunch. They'd secured a prime spot on the patio overlooking the glistening aquamarine waters of the Caribbean Sea.

Amber said, "Your article was great, Beanie. It's a crazy story, but you explained it pretty well."

Scoffing, Beanie said, "Yeah, I tried. It wasn't easy."

Fields laughed. "Oh, how hard could it have been to explain how a guy scammed four guys, then faked his death and fled the island, then returned to the island ten years later, then cheated on his girlfriend who decided to get back at him by telling one of the guys he scammed that he was still alive, and then that guy told the other three guys who got scammed that the scammer was still alive, and then … man, did I miss something?"

"Sounds like a complicated story to tell," said Amber.

Beanie said, "Basically, I think of it as a revenge and murder plot gone completely sideways."

"It's sad that Archie Hall killed three people because he lost money due to his own greed," said Noelle. "Some people will never take responsibility for their actions. It's always some outside force compelling them to behave badly."

"Archie Hall claims he had no choice," said Fields. "Janvier questioned him. The way Hall sees it, the blame lies with Zach Preston. If Preston hadn't scammed the men, nobody would be dead."

"Don't forget, Hall was planning to kill Tarragon Ungaro," said Beanie. "And me, too."

"I'd like to forget that," said Noelle.

Beanie took a sip of beer and glanced at the centerpiece—hibiscus petals floating in a glass bowl. Noelle's tone, a mix of fear and frustration, made Beanie feel like a rube. One of these days, he was going to stop putting himself in the line of fire. His wife had been devastated to learn he'd almost been killed. If not for Officer Fields' call to the St. Xavier police, Beanie might have been Archie Hall's fourth victim.

"Oh, and Janvier found out that Archie Hall got his wife involved in his mess," said Fields.

"How?" asked Beanie.

"She worked as a mail clerk at the post office," said Fields. "She called in the tip to the St. Killian police, telling them she was Preston's neighbor and saw him bury a gun in his backyard."

Amber asked, "Is she going to be charged with anything?"

"Possibly, but I'm not sure," said Fields. "The St. Killian prosecutors might want to bring some type of aiding and abetting charge against her. Or obstruction of justice."

"Because she helped Archie cover up a murder," said Beanie.

"What does she have to say for herself?" asked Noelle.

Fields shook his head. "A friend of mine on the St. X force says she lawyered up quick, and she's not talking."

"Shocking," quipped Beanie.

"Another person not taking responsibility for their bad decisions," said Noelle.

Fields said, "I'm starting to think twice about getting older."

Giggling, Amber playfully swatted Fields' arm. "Why would you say something like that?"

"Because it seems like, in the Palmchat Islands, at least, that when you get old, you go crazy."

Noelle shook her head and chuckled. "Well, Damon, that doesn't sound ageist at all."

"I get what Fields is saying," said Beanie. "The last couple of high-profile cases have involved senior citizens."

"There was Old Wilson, the serial killer groupie," said Fields, studying the menu. "And Luther Tindall, the insane former cult leader."

"And …?" prompted Amber, smiling at Fields.

"And …" echoed Fields, looking slightly confused.

"That was only two examples," said Amber.

"Two out of hundreds," said Noelle, taking another sip of her drink.

"Okay, so maybe not all the high-profile cases," said Beanie.

"But two is two too many," said Fields. "You get these crooks, like Archie Hall, who are supposed to be enjoying the twilight of their lives. But they're plotting, scheming, stealing, and killing when they should be spoiling their grandkids."

Beanie's thoughts drifted to evil grandfathers. Archie Hall, who'd learned to text from his grandkids, wasn't the only bad granddad. Lime Shoes was a ruthless PC-5 gangster. And, of course, Josue Chartres was the notorious hitman. Would Archie's grandchildren think of him differently, knowing he was a cold-blooded killer? Would they abandon and disown him? Withdraw their love from him? Or, despite his crimes, would they rally around him, choosing to support him, hoping to understand his descent into homicidal depravity?

"Are you guys ready to order?"

Beanie glanced up at the waitress, a young island girl with corkscrew curls and a bright, dimpled smile.

After everyone nodded, the waitress flipped open a small pad. As Noelle, Damon, and Amber listened to the specials of the day and posed questions, Beanie picked up his glass of water and took a sip, chasing the island brew.

On the other side of the table, Fields and Amber laughed and joked at each other's lunch choices.

How will it work? Wondered Beanie. A dedicated, dutiful police officer and the daughter of a notorious gangster. Noelle was pleased with her matchmaking, but Beanie worried Fields might get his heart broken. Or worse, his life might be threatened if he managed to break Amber's heart. What if Lime Shoes tried to force Fields into a compromising position? The PC-5 was known for recruiting police officers to function as gang moles. Sometimes those cops looked forward to going on the take. Other times, they were given a choice of doing the cartel's bidding or else.

Beanie sipped his Felipe beer.

Hopefully, the two wouldn't get serious but judging from the affection they exhibited toward each other, Beanie feared they might already be a couple.

Was that a twisty mystery, or what?

Nothing was as it seemed!

There were a lot of suspects and even more sinister secrets to uncover but once Beanie figured out the deadly motive, he discovered the killer.

Fourth of July brought a corpse in the sand dunes.

But the summer mayhem is not over!

Beanie takes his wife and kids on a relaxing vacation, but fun-filled sunny days turn dark and sinister when a horrible accident claims the life of a popular lifeguard.

At first, the terrible incident seems like an unforeseen tragedy, but soon there are accusations of malicious negligence.

In *Summer Vacation Murder*, you'll have to figure out …

Was the accident really an accident? Or was the victim murdered?

Summer Vacation Murder is the next cozy murder mystery novel in the Reporter Roland Bean Cozy Mystery series. With plenty of twists and turns, it will keep you guessing until the jaw-dropping ending that you won't see coming!

Get your copy of Summer Vacation Murder today!
https://geni.us/summervacationmurder

Are you eagerly anticipating Beanie's next unexpected detour into a mystery waiting to be solved?

Then **Beanie's Mini Mystery Moments** are for you!

Get an exclusive quick-read mystery that spins off from one of Beanie's mystery adventures delivered straight to your email inbox!
https://BookHip.com/XWNHAAX

ALSO BY RACHEL WOODS

SASSY SARCASTIC CAT COZY MYSTERIES

Sophie Carter, a struggling reporter for the *Palmchat Gazette*, teams up with a sassy talking Calico cat to solve crimes as she strives to become an influential investigative reporter

A SLY AND SINISTER TAIL

A COLD AND CALCULATING TAIL

A FOUL AND FRIGHTENING TAIL

A DARK AND DEVIOUS TAIL

REPORTER ROLAND BEAN COZY MYSTERIES

Roland "Beanie" Bean, husband and loving father, finds himself the unwitting participant in solving crimes as he seeks to make a name for himself as a reporter for the *Palmchat Gazette*.

HAPPY BIRTHDAY MURDER

EASTER EGG HUNT MURDER

MERRY CHRISTMAS MURDER

TRICK OR TREAT MURDER

GOBBLE GOBBLE MURDER

HAPPY 4TH OF JULY MURDER

SUMMER VACATION MURDER

HAPPY NEW YEAR MURDER

PALMCHAT ISLANDS MYSTERIES

Married journalists, Vivian and Leo, manage the island newspaper while solving crimes as they chase leads for their next story.

UNTIL DEATH DO US PART

NO ONE WILL FIND YOU

YOU WILL DIE FOR THIS

DON'T MAKE ME HURT YOU

THE PALMCHAT ISLANDS MYSTERIES BOX SET: BOOKS 1 - 4

RUTHLESS REVENGE ROMANCE SERIES

Gripping romantic suspense series with steamy romance, unpredictable plot twists and devastating consequences of deceit.

HER DEADLY MISTAKE

HER DEADLY DECEPTION

HER DEADLY THREAT

HER DEADLY BETRAYAL

MURDER IN PARADISE SERIES

A series of stand-alone women sleuth mysteries with murder, mayhem and a dash of romance, set against the backdrop of turquoise waters and swaying palm trees of the fictional Palmchat Islands.

THE UNWORTHY WIFE

THE SILENT ENEMY

THE PERFECT LIAR

ABOUT THE AUTHOR

Rachel Woods studied journalism and graduated from the University of Houston where she published articles in the Daily Cougar. She is a legal assistant by day and a freelance writer and blogger with a penchant for melodrama by night. Many of her stories take place on the islands, which she has visited around the world. Rachel resides in Houston, Texas with her three sock monkeys.

For more information:
www.therachelwoods.com
rachel@therachelwoods.com

ABOUT THE PUBLISHER

BonzaiMoon Books is a family-run, artisanal publishing company created in the summer of 2014. We publish works of fiction in various genres. Our passion and focus is working with authors who write the books you want to read, and giving those authors the opportunity to have more direct input in the publishing of their work.

For more information:
www.bonzaimoonbooks.com
info@bonzaimoonbooks.com